Crash & Burn

Be sure to get all of Amanda Reid's exciting stories, available exclusively through Amazon Kindle and Kindle Unlimited!

Flannigan Sisters Psychic Mysteries

(Small-Town, Cozy Mysteries)

Finders Keepers

Ghosts, Pies, & Alibis

Murder Most Merry

Fourth and Long

Ghosts, MOs, & a Baking Show

Last Rodeo

Enchanted Rock Immortals Novellas

(Paranormal Romance)

The Wolf Shifter's Redemption

The Demon's Shifter Mate

The Fae's Obsession

The Shifter's Savior

The Lion Shifter's Trust

The Gargoyle Dilemma

Crash & Burn

A Flannigan Sisters Mystery

Amanda Reid

Cover Art by Book Cover Insanity, at bookcoverinsanity.com

ISBN: 978-1-951770-08-2

For Robyn. You're made of awesome. Except for your big toe, and that had to go.

CHAPTER 1

Ding.

Sunny Flannigan stopped at the side of her truck and dug around in her purse for her phone. Finally, she found the device and looked at her text messages, this new one from her boyfriend, Cace Navarro.

'Lunch? Tipsy Burro? 12:30?'

She checked the time. Fifteen minutes from where she'd exited her dentist's office. Perfect. Her heart buoyed by the opportunity to grab a lunch with Cace, she tapped a simple 'thumbs-up' in response.

The lunch balanced out the not-so-exciting list of accomplishments on her day off. She hopped into her truck and pulled out of the parking area. A clean bill of health for her teeth, if not a slightly sore jaw from holding her mouth open and gums which still felt a bit violated. At least now she could take off the band-aid from where she'd gotten blood drawn for her physical—a preliminary clean bill of health there too.

Her stomach rumbled in anticipation of food while she folded the bandage and put the little wad in her truck's garbage bag. With the blood draw, she'd had to fast, which meant no breakfast. One of the Burro's chile rellenos would fill the empty space in her belly beautifully. And give her the fortitude to brave the masses for her appointment to renew her driver's license at two o'clock. Her mouth watering, she bumped up her turn signal to make her way to her favorite Belton restaurant.

Eight minutes early, she pulled into the restaurant's parking lot and spied a spot right by the door. Her parking karma was on today. To her left, across the U-shaped lot, a large black SUV pulled out from a slot near the exit. A Texas State University shield and stick-figure family lined the back window. The name 'Sherry' in pink camouflage print sealed the deal. The SUV belonged to Sunny's supervisor, Sherry Roundtree. Cary, a prosthetist she worked with frequently, sat in the front, while Malcolm and Chloe, both physical therapists, sat in back.

Dang. She missed her office's Taco Thursday at the Tipsy Burro. At least on her day off, Sunny didn't have to forego the tradition. Besides, lunch with her man would always beat lunch with her coworkers.

She guided her truck toward the empty parking spot she'd spied earlier.

A tingling started in her fingers.

She glanced at them wrapped around the steering wheel. *Not now.* She flexed her digits. Maybe she merely held the wheel too tight. The sensation grew as she approached the empty slot. *No. Not now.* Pin pricks swarmed to swamp her hands.

She huffed a breath through clenched teeth. *Dang Flannigan Gift strikes again.* Now she'd miss lunch with her boyfriend to go find something for the crazy psychic power. Why couldn't she have premonitions like her younger sister, Lacey, or see ghosts like her older sister, Mina? Something normal. Well, more normal than finding odd things that needed to be returned to the rightful owner.

Mumbling her disappointment, she continued past the beckoning empty spot next to the Burro's front door and continued around the u-shaped lot toward the exit. She reached into her purse for her phone, then pulled back when a nudge to her shoulder had her applying the brake. This far away from the front door, few vehicles dotted the parking area.

She threw up her hands. "What do you want?" Hangry had her talking to the silly paranormal Gift. "If I turn now, I'll run into the wall of the flower shop next door."

The nudge returned, indicating she should turn right. If the Gift wanted her to exit the parking area, her paranormal power would've had her continue forward. She pulled her truck into a parking spot near where Sherry had pulled out and cut the engine. Sunny wasn't about to ram the wall of the concrete block building in front of her, no matter how much her hands would burn if she didn't locate the item the Gift wanted her to find. Whatever had been lost would have to stay locked in there if it had fallen in one of the brick's holes during construction. Gah. No use speculating.

"What now?"

The pin pricks increased to burning. She must be near. *Whew.* Maybe she could still salvage lunch with Cace. She grabbed her purse and slid out into the windy, early October day. Her feet crunched on the gravel under her running shoes. No need to lock her door. No one wanted a fifteen-year old beater, even if she kept the truck in pretty good shape.

She took in a centering breath. Mindful others could see her, she kept her questions internal. *Which way now?* The Gift nudged her to the left, toward her pickup's tailgate. A sequence of shifting pressures against her shoulders brought her to the passenger side of her truck and she scooted down its length next to a Fiber-Now Cable company van. The pressure released just short of having to duck under the van's overlarge side mirror.

Sunny looked down to the rough gravel. *Dig?* She'd look pretty silly making sand castles in the parking lot, and she'd forgotten her plastic pail. Pressure grew on the tops of both shoulders. *There's nothing there.* The pressure increased. Great. She crouched down, still scanning. *I don't have anything to dig with.*

A nudge. To the left. A glint in the gravel under her truck. She reached, and her fingers grazed, yet couldn't grasp, the object. She'd have to get on her knees. At least the early autumn day wasn't too hot, and she'd chosen jeans.

Despite the denim covering, rocks still dug in painfully when she put her weight on her knees. She reached for the glint and grimaced. The twisted, awkward angle threatened a pinched shoulder nerve. There! She closed her fingers around something plastic, and she pulled herself from underneath her truck, then back to upright. The burning ceased as if the sensation had never existed.

Thank goodness. At least she'd still be able to have lunch with Cace. She glanced down at the object in her palm.

A…thumb drive? The device appeared innocuous—red plastic with silver banding the edges. Huh. She'd parked one spot over from where Sherry had been. Maybe one of her coworkers dropped the device. So much simpler if that were the case.

She slid the drive into one of her front jeans pockets and bent to dust off her knees. She'd ask tomorrow. If not, she'd undoubtedly cross the path of the person to whom the little storage device belonged. Correction, to where the item should go. The gun she'd found while on a three-day weekend with Cace in the spring had gone to the police, not to the owner. She shrugged. What harm could a thumb drive be? Like the innumerable earrings, keyrings, pens, purses and other objects she'd found over the years, her Gift would let her know where the storage device belonged.

"Hey, you. Got a tire problem again?" Cace said from behind her.

She pivoted with his voice and leaned forward to be enveloped in a hug. "Nope." She pulled back and followed him from between the vehicles. "Why are you eating this late? Don't you normally eat around eleven?"

He threaded his fingers with hers as they walked side-by-side to the door. "We had a burglary call right around eleven. I hoped you might be done with your dentist appointment." A grin crossed his tanned, handsome face, revealing straight white teeth a movie star would envy. "I got lucky."

"I don't know who's luckier. I'm going to lunch with the handsomest guy in all of Central Texas."

He knocked his shoulder against hers with an amused, "Uh huh."

She stepped through the door he held open for her and into The Tipsy Burro. Though busy, the hostess escorted them to a table. *Dang.* Across the dining room, her landlord's nephew and occasional handyman, Walter Randle, sat in a booth, talking to someone across from him. She hastily averted her gaze. No need for the guy to think she saw him. He'd always given her the creeps when they spoke, with his eyes lingering everywhere on her body except her face.

After seating them, the hostess returned seconds later with a loaded basket of chips and a bowl of the locally-famous salsa, then she took their drink order of two sweet teas.

Sunny snagged a chip and dug into the salsa. So darned good. She swallowed with a sigh of satisfaction.

The server approached the table and took their order. Neither Sunny nor Cace had looked at the menu. Chile rellenos for them both.

"Have you checked your email?" Cace asked.

She finished chewing her second tortilla chip. "Haven't had time. What's up?"

He shook his head, a small, satisfied smile on his face. "The District Attorney said Gwen Plumlee took a plea. They won't need us to testify at her trial."

Sunny hovered her hand over the chip basket, then pulled back when relief swamped her. She wouldn't have to face the woman in court. "I never would've guessed Gwen would take a plea. Maybe the gun tied with the diary entry sealed the deal and she had no choice."

"It all pulled together." Cace's shoulders lifted under the deep blue of his uniform. "They found her fingerprint on the trigger. I'd say you were definitely instrumental." He grimaced when the microphone clipped to his shoulder squawked. He reached down to his waistband, presumably to turn down the volume on the radio clipped to his belt. "Regardless, she's agreed to First Degree Murder and will spend the rest of her life in prison. No death penalty."

"Killing a Texas college football legend would not be a fact in her favor, even with the stories about the abuses he put his players through." Sunny's annoyance at public opinion ruined the buzz of not having to testify. Too many people had pushed aside those stories, choosing to believe in the coach's winning image, rather than the pain and devastation he'd left in his wake. At least the murder had reopened the discussion about head trauma, something

Sunny understood all too well from the patients she saw at the physical therapy clinic.

"Well. At least we can put that behind us." Sunny dug into the salsa with another chip. "And it's not like anything like that will happen again."

A shadow dropped over Cace's features. "I hope not. You've had too many close calls in the last year. First, Ben Moody kidnapped you, then Gwen tried to shoot you."

She stifled a sigh. When had the last lecture been? A month since he'd harped on how her Gift kept putting her in danger? At least the conversations were becoming less frequent with the distance from the incidents. She cocked her head, put her finger to her cheek, and squinted her eyes, as if searching for facts. "If memory serves me right, Ben kidnapped you, too, and Gwen actually shot at you."

His lips twisted. "My point is you need to be more careful."

"I know. Nothing's happened lately, though, right?"

"Right," he said after a pause. "However—"

"I'm careful. I've got my mace. I've been taking Krav Maga classes at the gym like you asked. I'm careful," she said again for emphasis. She appreciated his worry, though what more could she do? She couldn't ignore the Gift when the psychic ability wanted her to find something.

She covered his hand with hers and stared deep into his concerned brown eyes. "I promise not to put myself in those types of situations ever again. Cross my heart."

An echo in her mind finished the line. *And hope to die…*

CHAPTER 2

The next morning, Sunny swung around the corner of her supervisor's office, one hand in her scrub pocket fingering the little electronic storage device. Her manager sat at her desk, a puzzled crinkle knitting her forehead while she pulled at her earlobe.

No response from her Gift, no urge forward or tingling hands. Sherry must not be the owner. Rats.

Sunny turned to prepare for her first appointment, grateful she didn't have to endure another awkward conversation with her manager. Since her start at the VA physical therapy clinic included a federal investigation and Sherry having to put Sunny on administrative leave without pay, her relationship with her supervisor had been strained. For whatever reason, she'd never been able to build the same warm bond with Sherry like the rest of the physical therapists enjoyed. Sunny was included in group activities, yet not the camaraderie, which made her feel like a bit of an outcast.

"Sunny," Sherry said, with what sounded like a mouse click.

Dang.

When Sunny turned back, her supervisor had swiveled her chair to face the hallway. She fingered an antique locket strung on a fine chain around her neck.

"Good morning," Sunny said. "I was going to say hello, but you looked really busy." At least the excuse sounded good.

Sherry swiped a hand over the curls she tried to smooth down into a bun, yet the strands refused to remain tamed by whatever product she used. "I needed to talk to you anyway. It's that time again. Year-end evaluations." Her gloss-frosted lips curved into an ain't-this-fun smile. "I've shifted a couple of appointments on Tuesday, so be sure to check your schedule."

"Great." Sunny put as much enthusiasm behind the word as she could muster. An hour of 'accomplishments' and 'goal setting' for next year.

"I think…" Sherry's features twisted slightly, then she sighed. "I'll see you on Tuesday."

Unable to determine exactly what her supervisor's expression meant, Sunny sketched a wave, then continued down the hall toward the front desk and her schedule. Ugh. Evaluations. The mid-year meeting six months ago couldn't have been more awkward. Yet the stilted conversation resulted in a glowing review. She'd already started looking for another job, figuring Sherry wanted to get rid of her. Instead, she not only retained her position, but got released from her employment's probationary period on-time.

You should be grateful. The random thought popped in her head. Grateful? *Even if she doesn't like you, she knows you're a good physical therapist and still gives you good reviews.*

Huh. She'd never thought about their relationship in that way. Sherry could've tanked Sunny. *Perspective is everything.*

She scanned her appointments for the day. Her gaze landed on her last spot, Major Karena Moseley. Sunny's spirits lifted, because she'd never met a more determined person. A positive attitude and resolve could work wonders and sometimes even medical miracles.

Five appointments later, Sunny grabbed her waiting chart, then used her shoulder to prop open the swinging door to the waiting room. "Major Moseley?"

The woman stood swiftly and approached Sunny with a confident stride. If Sunny hadn't known the major had a trans-femoral amputation, she never would've been given a clue. Prostheses may have come far since the simple plastic leg Sunny's grandfather used, but she credited Major Moseley's resolve for her swift recovery more than medical advances.

"Last appointment, huh?" Sunny asked while she paced to the workout room. She'd miss the determined, sarcastic, very brave woman.

The white of the major's teeth shone bright against her dark skin. "Last one."

Sunny followed the major into the clinic's workout room. Three other veterans with various prosthetic needs were in the process of treatment with other physical therapists. The prosthetist, Cary, stood in a corner, fiddling with the elbow joint on an arm. He glanced up and waved in her direction.

"Let's go into Room One." Sunny flipped the sign next to the door to indicate the room was occupied. The major hoisted herself onto the room's exam table, so her legs dangled from the edge while Sunny closed the door behind them. Sunny motioned to Major Moseley's prosthesis. "Let's take a look at your leg."

"It's not my leg." Humor lit in the major's eyes, and she pulled up the opening of her shorts to reveal the socket fitted over the end of her thigh. "It's my *bionic* leg."

"You're awful spunky today."

"It's my last official appointment. I've got to give you my best."

"Har-har." Sunny removed the prosthetic, then the compression sock, and bent to examine the major's truncated thigh. "I honestly don't know if I've seen anyone do this well."

"You've only been working here for a year."

Sunny rose to her full height, pasting a feigned, thoughtful expression on her face. "True. Though you *are* the model patient. You've taken care of your scar, made sure to let us know when the socket rubbed. You do every exercise, follow my every edict without complaint. We're letting you go earlier than most would even dream. Every physical therapist is jealous you're my patient. You make me look good." She crossed her arms and released the grin she'd been restraining. "And I've got year-end evaluations next week."

The major batted her eyelashes. "Then I'm happy to have helped."

The door behind her opened, and Sunny spun to find Malcolm Tolliver entering the room. With his head turned, he spoke to someone behind him.

"Occupied." Sunny said with a curt snap, stepping in front of the major. Many people didn't like their limbs put on display, hence the private rooms.

Malcolm's head snapped around and color seeped into the light brown of his face. "Apologies." He quickly backed out.

Sunny turned back to the other woman. "Sorry. He's new. I guess he still isn't used to our marking system here."

"Who's that hottie?"

"Major Moseley," Sunny said with a *tsk*. The major was, as far as Sunny knew, still happily married to a former Army Ranger who treated her like a queen.

"I'm married, not dead."

Sunny chuckled. "His name is Malcolm."

"If he'd been my physical therapist, I'd still be *struggling* to walk with the parallel bars." After she put air quotes around her emphasized word, she fanned herself with her hand and rolled her eyes.

Malcolm, tall and fit, with neat dreadlocks pulled into a band at the base of his neck and pretty amber eyes, turned many heads in the PT clinic. Sure, he was handsome. He also had a girlfriend who worked as a phlebotomist in the lab.

"Yeah, but if you were struggling on the parallel bars, you wouldn't be well on your way to that three-year marathon plan. Year two is done—regular prosthetic. When is your appointment to get fitted for a blade? Last time we talked, you had applied to be a guinea pig for Ossocorp's new fitness model."

"Yep. They've got a new electric impulse system. So sophisticated it's beyond my little grunt brain to understand how they function. I'm hoping the model works out for me."

Sunny did too. Those systems were notoriously tricky and some never quite sync'd with the person wearing them. The major was one of the nicest people she'd ever met. Hard working. Maybe even would've moved up in the Army if her injuries hadn't called for a medical discharge. She deserved this break.

"If there's anyone who can get to a marathon, my bet's on you," Sunny said. "Now let's roll through your exercises. I'll be suitably impressed and cut you loose early."

"You bet." The quick grin returned. The major rolled

up her compression sock, refit her prosthetic, then followed Sunny into the workout room.

She hadn't been kidding. Major Moseley had dedicated herself to her rehabilitation and flew easily through the stretches and exercises. "And with that, we're done." Sunny handed the other woman a towel from the freshly folded stack in the corner, then bent to write her final notes in the chart. "All you have to do is keep this up, and I don't think I'll be seeing you here again."

From her periphery, Malcolm walked by, rolling his client in a wheelchair. At the physical therapist's waist, she caught a flash of red and silver. She paused, and her gaze narrowed on the thumb drive dangling from the keychain clipped to Malcolm's belt loop. It exactly matched the device in her pocket.

"I thought you had a boyfriend?" Major Moseley asked.

Sunny dragged her gaze away and found the other woman with her hands on her hips and an eyebrow cocked with snark. "What? I do. You know all about Cace."

"I know you aren't dead yet, either, but you might want to be more discreet."

"I-uh—" Sweet Baby Jesus. She thought Sunny was checking Malcolm out. "No. I just found something I think belongs to him."

"He's something alright." The major patted her on the shoulder. "I'm only giving you grief. You take care of you and that soldier of yours."

Sunny's awkwardness dissolved, replaced by genuine sorrow. "You know you don't have to be a stranger. You're welcome to stop by any time."

"I have a little secret." She passed Sunny a business card. "David is starting a barbecue joint."

The glossy rectangle displayed 'Ranger Barbecue' in

white, block letters against a green camouflage background. The 'Ranger' appeared to be similar to the curved military patch Sunny remembered from a uniformed soldier's shoulder. A pig snapping a smart salute finished the decoration, followed by the Temple address and telephone number.

"He's been catering for a while with really good reviews. We finally found the perfect spot to set up a permanent restaurant." She looked down, then back up to Sunny. "I hope we'll see you there sometime."

Sunny's heart swelled with the honor. "When do you open?"

"Tomorrow."

"Then get your hiney over to that restaurant—he needs your help." Sunny placed a hand on the woman's shoulder. "Of course I'll come. Rangers have a drive to succeed. I know his food will be excellent and he'll make the business work. Plus, he has a secret weapon in his corner. You."

Relief flooded the major's features. "Thanks. He's worried. I know he'll do great. Even without me. We'll see you soon." She strode from the workout room, barely a hitch in her gait.

Sunny pocketed the card, finished the notations in the chart, then slid the file into the tray for data entry. Maybe she and Cace could wander over for dinner tomorrow. What was the address again? When she pulled the card from her pocket, the thumb drive fell to the floor. She stooped to pick it up.

Malcolm. Shoot. The Gift hadn't given her a sign to give the thumb drive to him. Maybe he could tell her where he got his device and help her find the owner.

Sunny rounded the corner and found Cary at the

receptionist desk. He quickly signed off the computer and stood.

Rats. "Hey, have you seen Malcolm?"

Cary glanced up. "He left a couple of minutes ago."

"Dang." Now what?

"You need something?" His gaze turned curious. He pulled his keys from his pocket and started jingling them, a sure sign of his impatience to leave.

"No, I…I needed to ask him a question." Cheese and crackers. The speculation in Cary's eyes. He thought she and Malcolm… Nothing she could do now. "I'll wait until tomorrow."

"Tomorrow's Saturday."

"I'll catch up with him on Monday, then."

"He's off until Tuesday. He's taking Shay to a family wedding. Must be getting serious if he's taking her to meet his family." Smugness had entered his tone and his avid gaze studied her. "You want his cell phone number?"

Grr… She wasn't lusting after Malcolm, and Shay seemed like a nice lady. Sometimes Cary could be such a jerk. "No need to bother him on his vacation. I'll catch up with him on Tuesday. See you later."

Great. Nothing like a hospital to fuel the gossip chain. She grabbed her purse from her locker and headed for the employee exit, grumbling to herself about having to wait three days for Malcolm to return. Maybe the recipient wasn't him, and she'd come across the person this weekend, rather than hunting down the owner. At least she could get her mind off the device tonight. The Country Swing Kings were in town at Solomon's Dance Hall and she and Cace had tickets. Attitude much adjusted, she reached for her keys.

A fine tingling thrummed through her fingers.

CHAPTER 3

Good gravy. What now?

Sunny tunneled her empty fingers through her hair, stopping to remove them carefully after encountering ponytailed, not loose, strands. She patted the ruffled bits back into place with a grumble.

The nudge to her back said forward. Sunny's spirits sunk. How long would this take? She could miss the concert. Cace usually understood when her weird power had her sprinting in a direction to give something back. Missing the Country Swing Kings would disappoint them both. She refocused as the pressure in her back increased, now almost to the point of pain.

"Okay, okay," she said under her breath. She badged her way out of the VA Clinic and exited into the pleasant early evening. She'd parked her truck to the left, apart from everyone else, a habit she'd acquired when her tires were slashed in this same lot over a year ago. Wow. That long? She turned to make her way to the pickup. The pressure abruptly shifted, pushing her hard to the right.

Cheese and crackers. Sunny recovered her balance and

stopped for a moment. If anyone saw her awkward move, they may think her drunk.

Are you sure? Another nudge, a little gentler this time, said go right, away from her truck. *Silly Gift. Fine.* She pivoted and continued the opposite direction down the sidewalk. The pressure increased on her right shoulder. To ensure she didn't get run over, she looked both ways before she stepped onto the parking area's blacktop. No moving cars. No other people visible, for that matter.

Whew. She continued forward. Not that she was doing anything wrong. The pain in her fingers increased. She must be close.

A flash of the late afternoon sun winked off the gridded pavement ahead, on the second tier of spaces. Probably an earring or something. Thank goodness. She'd get to go to the concert after all.

Her fingers began to burn the closer she came to the silver and red item. The pulsing sting in her hands abruptly stopped, and she stared down at...another thumb drive. Same as the one she had in her pocket. She pulled out the device to make sure she hadn't lost the tiny thing. Yep. The same one laying on the pavement.

Stranger and stranger.

Sunny bent, picked up the storage device, then placed it next to the one she found the prior day. Exactly the same. A silver rim along the two sides and a silver button to push out the USB connection.

"What you got there?" a male voice asked from behind her.

She jumped and whirled, shoving her hand holding the devices in her pocket.

Cary sat in his low-slung sports car, leaning over the console to look out the open passenger window.

Geez he was quick. He must've left the building when

she went to retrieve her purse from the locker. *Act normal.* She pulled her hand out and brought a coin along. "A dime."

"Hey, guys. Y'all have a good evening," a female voice said from beyond Cary's car.

Brinna Diaz, one of the physical therapists Sunny worked with, had stopped on the sidewalk, then walked toward the vehicle.

"You too," Sunny said, still striving for a normal demeanor. "Got anything fun planned this weekend?"

Brinna's grin spread wide. "Yeah, my mom's birthday is Sunday, so we're going to have a cookout. You?"

"Going to a concert tonight. Cace works Sundays, so I'll probably take a pj day."

"I get that." Brinna's laugh pealed high and giggly, and she moved off toward her vehicle. "Have a good one. You too, Cary."

"Always do." He revved his engine and started forward with a small spray of gravel.

Ugh. Sometimes that man was such a jerk.

She put the dime back in her pocket. Oh no. She pulled out the two flash drives. Which one was the one she found in the parking lot today?

Does it matter? She blew out a heavy breath, then pocketed them both. If the Gift wanted her to find the people they went to, the ridiculous power would tell her which one to give back, no doubt. Maybe. Hopefully.

She tramped across the lot to her truck. At least she'd make the concert tonight. Unless the Gift sent her in another direction. *Nope. Think happy thoughts.* Her spirits lifted slightly when she pulled from her parking spot and made her way to the spacious one-bedroom apartment in Belton she now shared with Cace. Fridays were his day off, but he decided to pick up an overtime shift and should be getting home about the same time as she.

Her phone rang. From the Star Wars theme song, she didn't need to see the caller ID. She dug the mobile from her purse without breaking eye contact with the road. "Hey, Garrett."

"Hey, yourself," her brother-in-law said. "Did I catch you after work?"

"Headed home now. What's going on?"

"I'm going to be at the Belton convention center tomorrow and Sunday for a hardware trade show. Didn't know if you and Cace had some time to meet up for lunch or dinner on Saturday?"

"Cace's off tomorrow, let me check with him. Maybe dinner?" She found herself smiling with the unexpected treat. She didn't get to see Garrett all that often.

"Sounds like a plan."

"Mina's home with Jake?"

"Yep."

Owning two businesses, a hardware store and a restaurant, meant the couple rarely left town, let alone at the same time. Maybe for an afternoon, but a several-day trip meant he traveled solo. An idea popped into her head. "Hey, there's a new barbecue joint opening tomorrow. Supposed to be really good."

"It's a date."

As she tucked her phone away, she hoped the major's husband got it right. Since BBQ was practically the state food, though her sister would argue chicken-fried steak actually claimed the prize, bad brisket was an unforgivable sin. Nah. Sunny couldn't comprehend the major and her husband would offer anything other than a top-notch meal.

She pulled into the little gravel parking area on the side

of the giant Victorian. The house had been sectioned off into four apartments and the double-residential lot allowed for enough tenant parking. Huh. No Cace yet. Maybe he had a call late in his shift. Hopefully, he wouldn't be too late for the concert.

Her phone alerted her to a text. She checked the screen on the way into the apartment. *Late call. Should be home before 1830.* Weird how she'd seemingly conjured his message. His delay would give her time to shower and pretty up.

Once inside, she dropped her purse on the kitchen table. Ugh. Warm. Sometimes Cace turned up the thermostat before he left, but not usually this high. She checked the display on the wall. Eighty. For goodness sake. At the side, the digital display showed the unit set at seventy-four. Uh oh. She glanced to the wall near the high ceiling. Air still rushed through the vents. She stepped into the flow. Warm. Meaning the air conditioning probably wasn't functioning. To be sure, she turned the unit off, counted to ten, then turned the switch back to the 'cool' setting. Maybe she would get a better idea if her simple on/off trick worked if she moved closer. She climbed to stand with one foot on the couch's arm, the other on the back, her hand stretched toward the vent. No cool air.

When it rained, it stormed. First, the Gift today and now this. She reached for her phone and dialed her landlord. Sunny could've walked around the porch and rang the doorbell, though she doubted Ms. Randle would've heard the chime over the dulcet tones of her favorite crime drama's volume set at the top level. At least the insulation installed in the shared wall between the two first-floor apartments made sure Sunny never heard the television.

"Hello?" Ms. Randle asked, her voice barely discernible above the show blaring in the background.

"It's Sunny, Ms. Randle. From next door?"

"Oh, hello, Sunny. What can I do for you?"

Sunny opened the closet and pulled out a box fan Cace brought from his old apartment. The current temperature would require a bit more circulation. "My air conditioning doesn't seem to be working. It's eighty in here right now."

"Have you checked the thermostat, dear?"

Sunny tamped down her frustration. "Yes. I checked the setting. Then turned the switch off, waited a bit, and turned it back on. No dice."

The older woman huffed a breath. "Okay. I'll call Walter."

Even worse. Her nephew. "I thought he got a new job."

"He might be able to fix it."

Like he fixed her toilet? His 'fixing' seemed to be limited to banging a wrench on the pipes, asserting he'd fixed it, then Ms. Randle having to call a true repairman right after.

If Sunny didn't like her landlord so much, she'd argue for an air conditioning tech right away. Surely no harm would come if Walter stopped in to check. A real tech probably couldn't come by tonight anyway since her nephew was no AC repairman. "Fine. We're going to be out this evening. We have tickets to a concert.

"Oh, you and Cace are going to be going out? I'm sure you're going to look pretty."

As pretty as I can be in this hot, humid apartment. "Yes, ma'am. I wanted you to know Walter may come by and we may not be here, so he'll need your key." Though not thrilled with Walter in her apartment, the fact Cace had moved in gave her a sense of security.

"Okay. I'll let him know."

Sunny tapped the red dot on her phone's screen, then moved through the apartment to open windows. Screens gave her a modicum of security. At least some airflow might allow the dropping evening temperatures to cool off the apartment. Ah. A little better. Weather in Texas was notoriously arbitrary in October. Days could be ninety, or they could be in the forties. Tomorrow's forecast from the morning news said high eighties.

She emptied her pockets, putting her change and the two thumb drives next to her purse. Time to get ready for dinner and the Country Swing Kings.

She'd just finished twisting her long hair into a messy side bun when the front door opened. A glance at her phone said six o'clock. Cace wouldn't be home this early. Due to the heat, she'd been waiting to put on her jeans until the last minute. She yanked them on and raced barefoot around the corner to encounter Walter Randle standing in her living room.

He gazed toward her purse, his mouth gaping open slightly. The man stood a couple inches taller than her, carried about twice her weight, and had a good ten birthdays more than Sunny. Instead of his usual faded and stained heavy metal t-shirt and jeans and his hair pulled into an unkempt ponytail, Sunny gaped at the wonder of a cleaned-up Walter in a Fiber-Now cable uniform of a gray button-down with short sleeves and darker gray pants. He'd even cut his hair. He reached toward her purse.

Did he not see her? "Walter?"

He snatched his hand back. "Hey, Sunny." His gaze traveled her length, then back up, lingering mid-chest.

Cleaned up, but hardly changed. Yay. She crossed her arms. "You should've knocked." Well, she had the bathroom fan on. Maybe she'd missed the sound.

"Aunt Margie said you and Cace would be out, so I grabbed her key."

Sunny ground her teeth. He still should've knocked. "Fine. The AC is out."

"That's what she said." He ambled over to the thermostat on the wall between the living room and bedroom. His features scrunched, and he peered at the display "Did you turn the switch off, then back on?"

"Yes." She tried to control her nostrils' flare. She'd said as much to his aunt. Besides, she wasn't stupid.

He flipped the switch to 'off,' and the air rushing through the vents ceased.

"I tried that."

"Um hmm." He flipped the tiny switch to 'cool,' and air began moving through the vent again. He held up a hand toward the blowing air. "Huh. Doesn't seem to be cooling."

She counted backward from ten. "As I said, I tried that already."

He flipped the switch to the 'off' position once more. He turned and stared at her, saying nothing.

Sweet Baby Jesus, this guy creeped her out. She started to run through some of the techniques she'd learned in her Krav Maga classes. Imagining Walter knocked out on the floor made her feel a little more confident about him in the apartment.

He flipped the switch again, and hot air rushed out. "Well, I don't think it's cooling. I'll tell Aunt Margie and call the repair man." He came several paces in her direction.

Too close. He should be headed toward the door. Did he not understand the law of interpersonal space? She took a step back.

"Are you going to be home tomorrow?"

She struggled to control her breathing, and her heart

had begun a heavy thump. "*We* can be home most of the day."

He apparently didn't appreciate the emphasis on her use of 'we.' A subtle shift and he'd moved closer. "Okay." He pulled a small notepad bound with a top spiral and flipped open the cover. He readied a pen. "If you'll give me your phone number, I'll coordinate the AC repair. Luckily, this isn't their busiest time, so I should be able to find somebody for tomorrow."

Unease gripped Sunny because he blocked the front door, the closest way out. Her other option was the kitchen, though his position blocked that path too.

"Sunny, your telephone number?" Walter's eyes slid down yet again, probably to the barest hint of cleavage she'd revealed with her western snapshirt.

Her heart thundered in her ears.

Another step had her backed against the wall. He licked his lips.

She tried to remember a move—any move—to use on him, but she'd frozen, unable to even say a word.

He stepped closer.

CHAPTER 4

"Why don't I give you my number?" Cace asked from the front door. His tone fell hard, bordering on ugly.

Relief flowed through Sunny to see her boyfriend standing just inside the doorway. "Hey, baby." She had to dodge around Walter to cross the room to Cace. Her hands still shook, and she threaded them through his to stop their trembling.

He searched her eyes as if looking for any sign of hurt. They narrowed when he shifted his gaze to the other man. "I'll be happy to coordinate the repairman." He recited his number, which Walter dutifully recorded, despite the sour twist to his lips.

"Is there a time you won't be home?" A hint of surliness lingered.

Cace said, "We can be—"

"Garrett called, and he's in Belton for a trade show," Sunny said. "He wanted to know if he could meet us for lunch or dinner."

"Why don't we tell him dinner? That way, we'll have

the whole day for the repair, right…I'm sorry, what's your name?

Sunny swung her gaze back to her landlord's nephew, whose eyes darted away from her purse again. Cheese and crackers. Not like she carried a designer brand. Did he want to steal her wallet?

"Uh, Walter Randle. Margie Randle's my aunt. During the day for the repair sounds good." He flipped the notebook shut and tucked it, along with the pen, back into his breast pocket. "Hey I thought I saw you two at the Tipsy Burro yesterday."

"Yeah," Sunny said. She leaned into Cace. "I had the day off, and we met for lunch. Were you there?"

"Yeah, I met Aunt Margie. I don't get much time with my new job, and they're fast. I guess you didn't see me." He shifted a bit on his feet. Had he even looked directly at Cace? His beady little eyeballs had been everywhere else. "Well, I'll let you know tonight if I can get someone for tomorrow."

"Text me. We're going out." Cace turned to Sunny. "Speaking of, are you about ready?"

She nodded. "Just need my boots."

"Okay, then. I'll get changed, and we can go." Cace leveled a pointed stare at Walter.

Whose sights had strayed to her purse again. "Oh, uh, I'll let you know." He crossed to the door and let himself out. Sunny tracked him while he rounded the front of the big Victorian, then ran on her tiptoes to the bedroom door and peered out the window, where she made sure Walter continued out of hearing to his aunt's side of the house. Then she flew back and launched herself into Cace's arms.

"Thank you so much." She buried her face against his neck. A shudder crept down her spine.

Cace hugged her to him. "You're welcome," he murmured into her hair. "I don't want him in here with you alone again, if possible."

She pulled back and lifted her eyes to his. "Then I wasn't imagining things."

"Nope," he said, expression grim. "And the way he looked at your purse, he planned to lift your wallet after he assaulted you."

Thank goodness. "So, you noticed that too."

He dipped his chin.

"He's got a master key," she said. "From his aunt."

Cace's lips flattened, and a muscle jumped in his cheek. "Don't be in here without throwing the internal deadbolt. Even if you expect me home. I'll knock or call you to let me in."

Her gaze strayed to the blind deadbolt, which turned from the apartment's interior, with no ability to unlock it from the outside.

"Surely he wouldn't…?" Of course he would. He'd already entered her apartment without knocking.

"You know I don't put anything past anyone anymore."

The gravity in his features solidified her wavering doubts. Yes, Walter probably would come in without permission using the key.

"I'll have a talk with Ms. Randle about her nephew." Cace's grim tone promised frank talk.

"No." The word burst from her lips. He was among the last of the older woman's family and Sunny didn't want her to get upset. "I'm pretty sure he got your message and won't bother me again."

Cace shoved a hand through his hair. "You're a very nice person, Sunshine Flannigan. Women are often too nice, mainly because of a societal expectation. And sometimes that means you're too nice when you should be more assertive."

"What…Are you telling me I need to be more mean?"

"To guys like Walter, yes. He had you pinned in the corner."

"I was already figuring out the best way to escape." *Liar. You froze.*

"Would you have done it?"

"If he had made a move." *Could you have?* Her stomach curdled. *Maybe. Maybe not.*

"He already made his move. When he maneuvered you into the corner, he cut off your avenue of escape."

Bile rose, and she swallowed the acid, the corners of her lips tugged down with the bitter taste.

He took a deep breath and let the air out carefully. "I'm not blaming you. What I'm saying is he herded you into a corner. By the tension in your face, I could tell you were uncomfortable. And so could he, because he kept coming closer. I know you were trying to be nice, but you don't have to wait to tell someone to back off your personal space." He clasped his hands on her upper arms. "Baby, I want you to be safe."

Her frustration rushed forward, and she took several steps back, pulling away from his grasp. "So, his behavior is my fault?"

He dropped his hands to his sides. "No. That's never your fault. A woman should be able to be in her own home with a handyman and not have to worry about being assaulted. In fact, she should be able to walk naked down the street without worry."

He turned and propped his butt on the back of the side chair, his brow lifted from a deep furrow. "All I'm saying is you shouldn't be scared to speak up if someone is making you uncomfortable."

Good grief. Now he talked to her like a father. She propped her shoulder against the wall and suppressed an eye roll.

"I know this sounds like I'm preaching." He rubbed the back of his neck. "Maybe I am, though I don't want to. I've seen violence against nice women too many times in the year and a half on this job. Don't worry about his feelings or what he'll think about you. Even if the 'he' is me. If I make you feel uncomfortable, I want to know."

Her anger dropped away. Maybe he had something there, because she'd frozen when Walter pushed her into the corner. Not that she'd admit the fact to Cace. Did she take people's feelings into account too much? Probably. But never Cace. He'd always made her feel safe and loved. Well, except for that hiccup seven years ago when he enlisted and left her with a Dear Jane letter. Yet they'd started over, learned from their mistakes. He'd moved in four months ago. Barely a hitch. "You've never made me feel uncomfortable."

"I'm glad to hear that, but I'm serious. I would never want you to feel that way around me." He gave her a lopsided smile. "Promise me?"

She stepped between his legs and lowered her chin a bit to gaze into his eyes. "I promise," she said, then brought her lips to his. The sweet kiss tempted her to linger. She drew back, a sultry smile on her lips. "We can continue this later. We've got tickets, right?"

He groaned, swallowing hard. "Right. Let me grab a quick shower and get changed. Even though we've finally dipped to the eighties, I'm still hot under this vest." He pushed off the chair and headed toward the bedroom, reaching for the clasp on his duty belt.

Sunny pulled on her cowboy boots, the pretty brown ones with turquoise embroidery, which matched her plaid shirt with the same colors. Then she closed all the windows and locked them. The effect took hold immediately, the breeze coming through the screens had been cooler than inside. She kicked the fan up a notch and pointed the airflow into the bedroom where Cace dressed. Thank goodness she'd chosen to put her hair up tonight.

She snagged the two thumb drives from the kitchen table and secured them within a zippered pocket inside her purse. She never knew when the Gift would want her to return them, and it wouldn't do for them to slide out. She'd just have to go look for them again.

Cace emerged from the bedroom, fresh and handsome in his civilian clothes. "Hel-lo stranger." She added a wolf-whistle at the end for emphasis. The jeans molded to his muscled thighs like a second skin, and the patterned, button-down shirt framed his wide shoulders.

"Lookin' good yourself, lady." He came to her side and offered his arm. "Ready?"

She accepted his solicitous offer and slung her purse over the other shoulder with a saucy grin. "I was born ready."

Outside, Cace locked the door, turning the key twice. Weird. He'd never done that before.

Foreboding slid up her spine and settled between her shoulder blades. "It locked, right?"

His smile carried a hint of worry. "Yep. You secured all the windows, right?"

She nodded her head. "Down and locked."

"Good."

With the single clipped word, another shiver of apprehension ran up her back. She tried to dismiss the unease. They'd locked everything right and tight. No one would get in. She should enjoy their dinner and the concert.

Maybe she'd even encounter the person who should receive one of the thumb drives.

She hopped into the passenger seat of Cace's pickup, determined to have a good time with her favorite man and favorite local band.

CHAPTER 5

It had to be close to midnight when Cace guided his pickup into the gravel parking area at the house.

Sunny still bubbled a bit from the concert. The band never disappointed with their hybrid brand of country and swing. Cace guided her expertly around the floor, though there had been little space for any flourishes to their two-step. Didn't matter. Spending time with him was the important thing. The Country Swing Kings were merely a bonus. And the bacon cheese burger she'd had at Old Jody's before the show couldn't have been better with the fried okra she'd substituted. She'd need to run at least an extra mile tomorrow. Her taste buds said the calories had been worth the indulgence.

She shifted in her seat toward Cace. "Thank you for the wonderful evening." Her tone emerged breathy and her gaze dipped to the console where her fingers tangled with his. She lifted her lids to find a hunger equal to hers smoldering in his eyes. She leaned forward, eyelashes fluttering down, head tilting in anticipation he would meet her halfway. His breathing told her he was close, but his kiss never came. She peeked at him.

"You're welcome." His lips quirked, then he took her mouth in the kiss he'd promised earlier in the evening. Their mouths slanted, tasting, caressing. Her hands, as well as his, slid from hair to shoulders to grasping at clothing, impatient with the barriers.

Sunny pulled back, her heart thundering with the desire pulsing through her. "I think it's high time we took this inside." She didn't wait for him, yanking the door handle, knowing with zero doubt he'd follow.

He met her at the front of the truck and wrapped his arm around her shoulder. She walked under the comforting embrace to the front door. With hands steadier than her own, he inserted the key and turned. A muttered string of swear words escaped him, ones he'd probably learned during his seven year-stint in the Army.

Her heart stuttered. "What's wrong?" she asked when his arm slid away to push her behind him.

He withdrew the key. "It's unlocked," he said in a low tone.

Sunny's heart stopped, then started thumping again, this time in fear. "You locked the door when we left," she whispered. "You checked."

The streetlight at the corner of the house illuminated the hard planes of his face. He handed her his keys. "Go get in the truck and lock the doors. I'm going inside."

She clutched at his arm and whispered, "What if someone's in there? What if they've got a gun? We should call the police."

His hand covered hers. "I'm not going to call them until we know for sure." He shook his head. "I'm sure I locked it, but I could've been wrong. I should know if someone's in there as soon as I go in. I'd rather you be in the truck." His face softened. "Please?"

Nerves gnawed in her stomach. "Okay. I'm going to have my phone ready to dial 9-1-1."

"Good idea. Thank you."

She raced back to the pickup, fear clawing at her insides. Many police officers routinely carried a weapon while off duty. Not Cace. Even if he had, they'd been at a bar where one shouldn't be carried anyway. Phone in hand, she shut the truck's door and engaged the lock.

From her position, she could clearly view Cace and would be able to see someone if they ran out of her apartment.

He waited until she climbed inside his pickup, then threw open the door and rushed in. On her phone's screen, she punched 9, a 1, then another 1, and allowed her thumb to hover over the green dot which would complete the emergency call. Seconds stretched into what seemed like hours. Right when she was convinced something had gone wrong, Cace stepped back outside and motioned for her to come in.

She clicked the lock button on her phone and rushed back to him. "What took so long?"

"It only took a couple of seconds. I wanted to make sure no one hid anywhere."

"I know, but…" Words clogged in her throat, caught in her worry.

He took her trembling hands in his. "Baby, if I had truly thought someone remained inside, I would've run back out right away. My gun is locked in the security container. I couldn't win that fight."

"Oh. Okay." She drew in a shaky breath, because he couldn't outrun a bullet. "Let's go inside. Please."

Once across the threshold, she scanned the rooms—living, dining, kitchen. Nothing appeared out of place.

Hardly the work of a burglar. She should know. Last year, her house had been ransacked.

Once he'd closed the door behind them, he threw the blind deadbolt, then tested the lock by pulling on the door, ensuring no one could enter from the outside, even with a master key.

Her thoughts drifted back to this evening, a sourness in her stomach. "You don't suppose Walter…"

"I don't know." He shoved a hand through his dark brown, wavy hair. "I would swear on a stack of Bibles I locked the door. Other than you and me, who has a key?" His expression said he specifically suspected Walter.

"Why would he do this?"

Cace paused, an inscrutable expression on his features. "He seems a little obsessed with you. I think you should check the apartment to make sure nothing's missing." He moved across the living room and started turning the blinds. Something they only ever did in the bedroom.

Her mouth dried. Good gravy. She put her purse in her usual spot on the dining table and surveyed the space. To her right, the kitchen, to her left the living room. Start in the bedroom, since most of her valuables, a couple of pieces of gold jewelry and her laptop, were there. All accounted for. Next to the kitchen. Cupboard after cupboard showed cup, plate, and pot all accounted for.

"Nothing missing here," she said to Cace, who'd leaned against the counter of the breakfast bar. "Why would he want a pot anyway?"

"You never know. He's pretty weird."

"Point." The only thing besides the table and chairs in the dining area was a flower centerpiece, so she moved on to the living room. Furniture and pillows all in place. "Everything seems to be here."

"Everything? All your decorations? They're here?"

What would he want with some books and knick-knacks? Two paintings on the wall she and Cace bought at an art fair not long after he moved in? Check. Television over the fireplace? Check. She crossed the room to her book case. Books, check. Granma's chocolate service. Check. Pictures. Check.

She turned and her gaze snagged on a shelf. She froze.

There should've been a picture in the empty space. Instead, a thin rectangle of shiny wood stood out against the light layer of dust. She whipped around to Cace, who hadn't left his position, merely shifted to observe her.

"There's a photo missing."

"Which one?" he asked through clenched teeth.

"I…wait. Let me think." She tried to visualize where the frame sat. The last time she remembered rearranging the shelf was four months ago, when Cace moved in. She'd accommodated some of his possessions. A memory nagged at her.

Oh, no. Bile rose in her throat and she shoved the acid back down.

"A picture of you and me at Jaime and Renee's pool party used to be right there. I remember because I didn't want to put it next to the picture of your grandmother."

Puzzlement crossed his features. "Why not?"

"That bikini is…small."

"Ah ha," he said with a quirk to his lips. "Well. Then let's see if there's anything else missing.

She finished the living area. "Nothing else I can find." She pushed a strand of hair from her face with an impatient hand. "I wish I didn't keep my drawers such a mess. The whole U.S. Army could rummage through them, and I'd probably never know."

"Well, now we know he has a picture of you in a bikini." Cace crossed his arms, his expression curiously bland.

No anger. No frustration. The mask must be covering his true feelings. "It's unusual for someone to target a woman who lives with a man. I don't like this, Sunny."

Her insides crawled with revulsion. How dare Walter violate her this way?

"We need to talk to Ms. Randle in the morning," Cace said.

"I think you're right." Great. Not that she had another option. Walter had obviously become a stalker. She wrapped her arms around her middle as cold swept through her, despite the lingering warmth in the apartment from the lack of AC. Memories, snapshots of last year's kidnapping, blew through her mind, stealing her breath.

Cace crossed the room and embraced her. No passion, comfort only. She leaned into his safety, pulling what heat she could to her suddenly frigid, shivering body.

Once her shaking had ceased, Cace pulled back. "You're going to be fine. No more Miss Nice-Lady. You've got your self-defense spray. You've been taking Krav Maga classes. You'll know what to do if he confronts you."

She nodded, her lips sealed against the howl of 'Why me?' threatening to escape.

He exhaled a sharp breath through his nose, then his features softened. "Come on, let's hit the hay. We've had an interesting night."

Minutes later, Sunny slid into bed next to Cace, the solidity of his body an anchor to her stormy thoughts. He wrapped his strong arm around her middle. Soon, his even breathing said he'd drifted off. For her, sleep remained more elusive.

The creepy feeling of being watched wouldn't let her go.

CHAPTER 6

Sunny swigged the last of her third cup of coffee. Usually, she only needed one in the morning, but a virtually sleepless night, starting at every little sound, had her already jonesing for a nap at only nine o'clock in the morning.

Yet, a jitteriness bounced through her, one which would deny her the sleep she craved. The buzzing wasn't due to the half pot of coffee she'd consumed this morning either. Lack of sleep had a way of making her full of nervous energy.

Cace, on the other hand, appeared to have experienced a blissful, full-night's rest, a role-reversal for them. He glanced up from his phone, where he'd been scrolling, then set the device on the table. "You sure you don't want me to tell her?"

"No. Ms. Randle should hear the news from me."

"Okay. The repairman should be here between one and three. Did you let Garrett know when we wanted to get together?"

Cheese and crackers. "I forgot all about him. Shoot, let me call." She pulled her phone. When Garrett didn't answer, she left a message after the prompt apologizing for getting back to him so late and stating that she and Cace would like to meet for dinner. After she hung up, she said, "I'd like to go to a restaurant. Today is their grand opening."

Once she'd described Ranger Barbecue and the owners, Cace said, "Great idea. Even if Garrett ends up making other plans, we should go."

And that's why she loved him so. Well, part of the reason.

He swigged the last of his coffee and put his cup in the dishwasher. "If it's okay, I'll go with you on your run after we see Ms. Randle."

She smoothed her running shorts over her hips. He hadn't gone on a run with her in a while. With narrowed eyes, she asked, "Are you joining me because of Walter?"

As he passed the kitchen table, he dropped a kiss on the top of her head. "Do I need a reason to spend time with you?" He continued through the living room and into the bedroom.

True enough. She let out a breath, determined to take him at his word. While she worked regular days at the clinic, he worked the evening shift, not returning until after midnight. A sleepy hello and a kiss were his normal welcome home. And since they had one common day off, they typically made the most of their Saturdays. Between last-night's burglary and Walter, she needed to work off some calories and a lot of jitters. Plus, she'd appreciate having him near.

Cace emerged a few minutes later. He carefully locked the door, then tested the knob to make sure the external deadbolt functioned. Cace tucked the key into the zippered side-pocket of his running shorts.

During the short walk to the other side of the house,

Sunny's nerves ping-ponged around in her gut. *Ugh.* She rubbed the fabric of her tank top over her belly. She shouldn't have had that third cup of coffee on an empty stomach. Exercise probably wouldn't make her roiling tummy any better.

She pushed the doorbell. By the television blaring through the walls, Ms. Randle had to be awake by now. Would the woman hear the chime over the—Sunny cocked her ear—reruns of that Navy crime show she loved so much?

Movement blurred behind the glass. The curtain on the grand door's sidelight shifted, then locks turned. The door swung open to reveal Sunny's diminutive landlord. She blinked and the eyebrows she'd drawn on climbed above the owlish glasses perched on her tiny, button nose.

"Good morning, you two. What can I do for you?"

Sunny peeked at Cace from the side of her eye, relieved to find him looking directly at her, allowing her the lead. "Do you mind if we come in for a moment? There's something I'd like to talk to you about."

"Sure, sure." Ms. Randle stepped aside, then led her and Cace to the kitchen. "Coffee?" she asked.

Though her stomach rebelled at the idea of more acid, Sunny said, "Thank you." Cace echoed her response.

Ms. Randle shuffled over to a cupboard while Sunny and Cace settled at the kitchen table. A quick glance around showed family photos lining the walls above shelves crammed with knick-knacks and more pictures. Sunny stopped her scan, then went back to one of what appeared to be a younger Walter flanked by Ms. Randle and who had to be her late husband. Probably Walter's high school graduation, since he had a diploma in hand, wore the mortarboard and gown, as well as an excited smile on his face.

She looks so proud. And I'm about to say something about him she may not like.

Ms. Randle put steaming mugs of coffee on the table before her guests. She gestured toward a tiny pitcher and a bowl of glistening white cubes. "Cream? Sugar?"

"Thank you, ma'am," Cace said.

Sunny doctored her coffee with both the cream and sugar while she grappled with how to tell her landlord she suspected her nephew of stalking. She took a sip. Oh, wow. That stuff could strip paint. Her stomach grumbled. More coffee had definitely been a bad idea. She set the mug with careful precision on the daisy-strewn, plastic table cloth.

Ms. Randle's face screwed up. "You look like you have bad news. Did y'all come to break your lease? You've got three months left." The index finger she wagged said she wouldn't forgive the two-months-notice and forfeiture of deposit provision for leaving early.

"No, ma'am. I'm not here to break the lease." *At least not right now.* "I needed to let you know of an encounter I had."

The old woman folded her arthritis-gnarled hands together atop the table. "This doesn't sound good."

"Well, I…" *You asked Cace to let you tell Ms. Randle. So do it.* Sunny took a deep breath. "Yesterday, Walter came over to look at my—our—AC."

"Right," her landlord nodded. "You called me, and I sent him. He said he couldn't do anything and would call the repair man. He said he talked to you both about scheduling."

"He did. He texted Cace to say the repair man would be here between one and three." Sunny's gaze dipped to the rocket fuel Ms. Randle called coffee before summoning the nerve to go on. "It's what happened prior to Cace coming home. Walter didn't knock on the door, and I wasn't dressed yet."

In her peripheral vision, Cace's fingers clenched around the coffee mug. Guilt curled in her stomach to curdle the coffee. She hadn't shared that little tidbit with him.

"Didn't knock?" Ms. Randle's vibrant, coral-tipped fingers fluttered to the bodice of her orchid-covered smock. "Oh, goodness. I told him he needs to. I've never gotten another complaint from any other tenants."

"Your other tenants are men," Sunny said, managing to keep sarcasm from her tone. "When he asked me for my telephone number, he began to crowd me into a corner. I was very uncomfortable. I tried to tell myself he wasn't threatening, but when I'm envisioning which self-defense move I'm going to have to use to get out of the situation, I know I'm not imagining things." She tried shaking off the horrible scenes replaying in her memory, yet they clung like cockleburs in her hair.

Ms. Randle's lips compressed, accentuating the deep grooves around her mouth.

Cace covered her hand with his where it lay on the table. "Fortunately, I came home and Walter backed off."

Sunny squeezed his hand, grateful for the support. "But after we came back home last night from a concert, the door was unlocked, and I found something missing from our apartment."

Ms. Randle's watery blue eyes stared back at her for several moments before she said, "What's missing?" Her words carried a hint of dread.

"A picture of me and Cace. I'm-I'm in a bikini." Would the older woman judge?

Ms. Randle's lips compressed more, until the vibrant

coral completely disappeared. "I'm sorry, Sunny. We—I—thought he'd gotten over his problem."

Sunny's heart thumped hard, and she massaged her chest. "What problem?"

"He's been in trouble for being a pest with women before. That was fifteen years ago, when he was much younger. I didn't think he'd start up again." Concern laced her sentences.

Relief her landlord believed her warred with unease the man had a pattern.

"Did he return the key to our apartment last night?" Cace's gentle words belied his tight grip on Sunny's fingers.

"He did." She pointed to a rack of keys on the wall over her shoulder.

Three sets of keys for the other residences in the house hung in neat order on hooks, including a set marked 'Sunny.'

Thank goodness.

"Right away?" Cace asked with a deceptively casual tone.

Ms. Randle's face paled under her heavy layer of powder. "No. I had to call him. He said he forgot, and he came back with them."

"How long did he take to come back?" Sunny stomach sloshed around the bitter brew she'd ingested, and she suppressed a grimace.

"About an hour." Her landlord's voice trailed off.

Enough time to go to a hardware store and make his own key.

"If you approve, I'm going to install a new lockset on the door," Cace said. "I appreciate you sharing with us your nephew's problems. I didn't want to have to break the news to you that he has a history of stalking women."

Sunny smothered a gasp and whipped her head to

stare at him. He knew and hadn't told her?

Ms. Randle sighed. "I guess you looked him up in the police computer?"

"No. I subscribe to a background service. Using the database at work would be illegal. I don't get the full information, though enough had been reported on there to concern me."

Sunny bit back the zillion questions on the tip of her tongue. First of all, why hadn't he told her?

"If you could put the new key where he wouldn't be able to find it?" Cace continued.

The landlord dipped her chin. "Certainly."

A fine vibration began to build in Sunny's fingers, not unlike when her Gift wanted her to find something. Except this time, no burning tingles, the she-needed-to-give-this-to-someone signal from her Gift. At least she'd brought the thumb drives with her, secured in the tiny, waterproof pocket built into her running shorts. She tunneled her fingers under the elastic. One was supposed to go to Ms. Randle? Maybe when she'd been at The Tipsy Burro with Walter she dropped the drive. But which one?

When she found the two devices, one had grown warm. *Thank you.* She palmed the tiny warm item in her hand and returned her attention to her landlord. "Thank you for believing me. Sometimes people don't want to imagine something like that happened."

A small, sad smile appeared on Ms. Randle's face. "Me and Bob couldn't have kids. We kind of adopted Walter at the age of twelve, when his mother died in a car accident. I loved that boy. It's a little harder to love the man he's become. I wanted to help him out by paying him to be my handyman until he found a job. Now that he's with the cable company, I think I'll let him know his services are no longer needed."

Sunny's heart nearly broke for the woman. She loved her nephew. "I'm so sorry."

"It's not your fault, honey. You tell me if you have another problem with him again. And save your receipt. I'll pay for the lock." Ms. Randle patted Sunny's hand, the one which concealed the flash drive.

"Oh, that reminds me. I found this computer thumb drive the other day, and I think it's yours." She put the small, red-and-silver device on the plastic tablecloth in front of her landlord.

She squinted down at the drive. "Mine? Oh, I don't think so. I don't use these things often. Though, I did have one like this not too long ago. Where did you find it?"

"In the parking lot outside the Tipsy Burro on Thursday. Next to a blue Buick like yours." Sunny suppressed a wince at the blatant lie. The gift demanded Ms. Randle should be the recipient, though she seemed to need convincing. What she did with the thing afterward was her own business. "Walter said you and he had lunch there."

"Oh. Okay. Thank you, dear." She picked up the plastic rectangle and stared at it through her glasses. With a small shrug, she dropped the thumb drive into one of the patch pockets sewn onto her outrageously orange orchid smock.

Sunny pushed her chair back and stood. "We're going to go for a run, then grab the lockset. We'll be back before the repairman arrives. Thank you for the coffee."

Cace joined her, and she walked hand-in-hand with him down the front walkway.

Sunny's steps felt light. Whew. Not only had Ms. Randle believed her about Walter, but she'd managed to deliver on one of her Gift's finds.

The day couldn't get any better.

CHAPTER 7

Mercifully, the door remained locked when they returned from their run, and further still locked when they returned from the hardware store with the new lockset. Sunny carefully scanned the rooms, looking for any additional missing items. Then she checked her straightened underwear, since all the television shows said creeps went there to steal women's panties. Nothing seemed to be out of place, including the hair she'd put on the edge of her unmentionables drawer. Thank goodness.

She reopened the windows. A pleasant cross-breeze blew from the bedroom to the living room, then out through the open portal in the kitchen. Though the day wouldn't be hot by Texas standards, the upper-eighties were forecasted for the area. No need to let the temperature build inside the apartment. She joined Cace at the kitchen table, where he rummaged through his toolbox. He'd already opened the lock's clear packaging and set out the pieces. The directions lay unfolded next to the brass and rubbed bronze components.

"Can I help?" Luckily, he wasn't one of those I-can-do-it-myself-kind of guys.

"Maybe. At this point, I'm going to get out the tools they say I'm going to need and read through the instructions. After that, I'll check YouTube for a video. I may be a minute."

"Okay. I'll take a shower."

She pulled the thumb drive from the little pocket and put it on the kitchen table next to her purse.

"I thought you gave that to Ms. Randle?" Cace's gaze narrowed on the red-and-silver object.

Cheese and crackers. Guilt seemed to be her default emotion today. "I found it in the parking lot yesterday after work. With the whole Walter-air-conditioning thing, I guess I forgot. I'm sure the Gift will let me know, like with Ms. Randle."

"Your Gift?" The tone, carefully stripped of all emotion, said he wasn't happy.

Good grief. "Yes. It has me find a lot of things. A lot more than I tell you. Keys. Necklaces, earrings. Even pens. Photographs. A marble once. Relax." She picked up the device and the silver flashed when she waved it in the air. "It's a harmless thumb drive."

He rubbed the back of his neck. "Sorry, sweetheart. This Walter thing has me on edge. I'll feel better when the lock is in and the air repaired so we can shut the windows."

"I understand. I'm concerned too." More like a lot concerned. She'd done some reading last night when she couldn't sleep. Escalation of stalking behavior worried her, something she decided not to tell Ms. Randle.

His gaze returned to the drive. "Why didn't you check what was on the devices to see if you could find who they belonged to?"

"I thought to, but one, I would feel like I'm invading their privacy, and two, they could've had a virus. I didn't want to have to buy another laptop." She put the red-and-silver item under discussion next to her purse. "Which reminds me." She crossed her arms, favoring him with a stare. Two could play at the interrogation game. "When did you look up Walter, and when were you going to tell me he has a criminal history of stalking?"

Cace rubbed the back of his neck. "This morning. I didn't want to alarm you, before I could confirm the information. Sometimes those sites match criminal histories with the wrong person, like credit bureaus get the wrong social security number and mess up your credit. Once I had confirmation from Ms. Randle or through more checking, I would've told you. You know that."

She searched his features and detected no deception. Mollified, she said, "Umm hmm. I'm going to shower."

Since the windows were open and they lived on the first floor, she took her clothes with her to the bathroom. At least that's what she told herself. She could've turned the blinds and dressed in the bedroom. The eerie feeling of being watched stuck with her, though. Stupid paranoia. Walter had her all cranked up.

As she finished drying off, a chime from her phone let her know she had a text. She threw her wet hair into a ponytail, climbed into her shorts and t-shirt, and searched out her mobile. A message from Garrett previewed on the screen, and she typed a response.

She returned to the living room to find Cace standing virtually where she left him earlier. "Garrett's coming here around six for a beer and a visit before we go to the restaurant," she said.

He glanced up from his phone with a slight frown. "Hope they have the air fixed by then."

Shoot. She hadn't considered that. "Fingers crossed." She glanced down at the table. The number of screwdrivers, the weird hexagon stick things, and other tools had expanded. She didn't doubt his DIY prowess, though. "Let me know when I can help."

"It looks strangely easy. But, I want to make sure I've got everything I might need."

Was that a little doubt in his tone? She patted his shoulder. "You are the best at figuring out puzzles. This can't be any worse."

"I think I'm ready. I'll take your help."

She moved to the other side of the door and onto the porch like he requested when the spooky, watched feeling returned. She glanced over her shoulder.

Walter stood on the porch about twenty feet away at the front corner of the Victorian. Not in his cable uniform this time, rather he wore an old high school football t-shirt and jeans. When she'd turned, his face smoothed from derisive to neutral.

A shiver ran down her back. He came forward, stopping at a respectful distance. "Sunny, Aunt Margie said I made you feel uncomfortable. I wanted to apologize."

The way he said 'uncomfortable,' as if he'd motioned air quotes around the word, made Sunny's eye twitch. If he'd uttered a sincere apology, she'd just won the lottery. And she hadn't even bought a ticket.

"Thank you," she said simply. No apologies from her. He needed to leave.

His eyes shifted to Cace, who'd risen from his crouch and exited the apartment to stand at her side. Walter's mouth pinched. "You're putting in a new lock?"

"Yes." Cace's single word held a palpable menace.

Walter cleared his throat. "Well, let me know if you need any help," he said, his voice strained. He disappeared around the front side of the house.

Their bedroom was in the front part of the house, the old parlor.

She raced into the apartment and into the bedroom. A form which appeared to be exactly like Walter stood silhouetted in the window. Rage lashed through her. This man would not intimidate her. She rushed forward and pushed aside the sheers to come face to face with the sneering man.

Without breaking eye contact, she shoved the window down and locked the sash. "Leave me the hell alone," she said, packing as much fury into the words as possible, then turned the blinds shut and yanked the sheers together.

"Are you okay?" Cace asked from the bedroom doorway. Despite his gentle question, his stare through the window would've burned a hole through Walter.

She stuffed her fists on her hips. "Absolutely. Miss Nice Lady has decided she's had enough of Walter Randle."

CHAPTER 8

Garrett arrived a bit later than originally planned. Apparently, hardware retail conventions were busier than Sunny would've imagined. He still wore his convention badge over his Shaffer Hardware polo shirt and came bearing hostess gifts, if pretty, patterned duct tape, superglue, and a basic tool set for a car could be considered as such. Especially when she suspected they were giveaways. Nice giveaways, though.

"How're Mina and Jake?" Sunny's stomach growled a demand for food while they piled into Cace's truck to head to Ranger Barbecue.

"They're good," Garrett said. "Jake's growing faster than Johnson grass. I can't believe he's in third grade already. And Mina, well, after the whole Pie Masters Challenge disaster, business is booming. People want to come meet the woman who avenged Camryn Nicholson's death. So much so, she's been able to hire another full-time cook and give the staff a raise. The strangest thing is…I think she's considering opening up a ghost investigation business."

If Sunny had been driving, she would've wrecked. Growing up, Mina had always denied her gift, and only recently let a few know of her talent to see spirits. "Holy cheeseburgers. A detective agency."

"Shh." His eyes darted from side to side, as if checking no one would overhear him. "Don't tell her I told you. You can say the Flannigan Gift let you know or something."

Cace chuckled.

"Y'all don't start ganging up on us Flannigans now," Sunny said with mock severity. "But seriously. What do you think?"

"I think she can do whatever she wants. The Cup and the hardware store are doing really well. Since Brittany came back to work, she started back to school to get a marketing degree and I think she'll be an excellent assistant manager. I should be able to work normal hours soon. Did you know she had two years of junior college? All she needs is two more years, well, about another year, and she'll graduate."

"Didn't she steal from you?" Cace's brow furrowed. "I thought you prosecuted her."

"She did. I understand why. I asked for her to receive deferred adjudication. If she finishes her probation, the conviction will be expunged. I think she's a good girl who made a really stupid decision. Well, two. One to have a baby and tie herself to Wayne Beedy, and the other to steal, rather than come to me when she fell behind because he never made child support."

"You're a nice guy, Garrett Shaffer," Sunny said. Mina was the most ornery of her two sisters, and Garrett's consistent devotion to her amazed everyone in their home town of Dew Drop, Texas.

"Hey, it's easy when you're married to a Flannigan."

Sunny rolled her eyes. "Suck up."

Both Garrett and Cace chuckled, and they the rest of the drive flew by, consumed with good-natured ribbing.

In no time, they were pulling into the restaurant's parking lot, old and strewn with potholes. Not packed with cars, yet a respectable crowd for a business on opening day. Good for the Moseleys.

Sunny stepped out of the truck and surveyed the freshly-painted building, what had once undoubtedly been a pizza franchise by the roof's distinct shape. Now the façade sported a big sign declaring the business to be *Ranger Barbecue* in the same military BDU colors, font, and pig shape as on the card Major Moseley gave Sunny yesterday. Red, white, and blue plastic pennants had been draped from each of the building's corners to light poles at the edge of the road, and a giant 'Now Open' banner hung underneath the main sign.

Garrett stood next to her and barked a laugh. "The pig is funny. If the brisket is as good as the sense of humor, we're in for a treat."

Cace held the door for her. Once inside, the smell of oak smoke and barbecue meat hit her. Her stomach rumbled with anticipation. Next, she scouted the layout. A typical, old-school-Texas barbecue joint. Customers ordered from a counter and took away their food on butcher paper atop a tray. A modest line of customers said this would be a good day. Major Moseley, wearing jeans and a black Ranger Barbecue-branded t-shirt, greeted customers near the door. Sunny's heart swelled with the other woman's tall, proud stance.

The major's face lit up when Sunny approached. "Thank you for coming," she said, enveloping Sunny in a tight hug, then surveying the two men behind her. "Who did you bring with you?"

After Sunny made the introductions, the major gave

her the side-eye. “My name’s Karena. Not Major Moseley. I no longer answer to that, I’ll have you know.” The entrance door opened to admit more patrons and Karena said, “Go get in line. I’ll come talk once y’all’ve sat down.”

David Moseley, the former Ranger, carved the meat behind the counter. His ready smile and desire to make Major—Karena—happy had always endeared him to Sunny.

When she selected her meat entree, she made introductions again, briefly this time, to not knot up the line. Soon enough, she sat at a four-top table between her boyfriend and her brother-in-law, an array of succulent, juicy meats on the tray in front of them. For sides, they’d selected a ‘twice-baked-potato salad’, green beans sprigged with bacon pieces, and coleslaw. A pile of plain white bread, a Texas barbecue tradition, sat stacked on the side. She selected half a sausage link, a slice of turkey breast, and two slices of beef brisket rimmed with a gorgeous, pink smoke ring. David supplied two sauces, mild and spicy.

Sunny quelled the desire for her knee to start bouncing while she waited for Cace and Garrett to finish serving themselves. Finally, her fork met beef, and brought the morsel to her mouth. Flavor exploded on her tongue, beef, smoke, and whatever magic he used to make his rub. Because he had to be a wizard. The spice melded perfectly with the meat and smoke. Heaven. “Wow,” she whispered.

“I know,” Cace said, his voice slathered with awe.

Garrett nodded while chewing his bite of brisket, his eyes rolling heavenward.

Next came the sauce testing. The mild, a tomato-based traditional with a twist she couldn’t quite identify. The spicy, though, held the right amount of heat. Not enough to break a sweat on her brow, but the right level to make her taste buds sing. Every morsel on the tray disappeared in record time, with a debate on going back for another container of the potato salad. She'd never had the dish made that way. The cheese, bacon bits, sour cream, and green onion couldn't have worked together better.

The clatter of silverware on the floor sounded behind her. Had someone dropped their tray? She turned and found Cary reaching down toward the floor from his seat behind her.

"Cary? Hey. I didn't know you were here too." Dumb comment. She sat with her back to the main doors, so no wonder.

He continued on his path until he'd retrieved his fork, which had landed near where she'd set her purse on the floor. He rose and said in a strangled voice, "I didn't notice you either."

As she was about to introduce him to Cace and Garrett, who were holding a conversation about the merits of the new coach hired by Texas University, Cary patted his pocket, then pulled out his phone. "Oh, hey, I've got to go. Bye."

He got up from the table with a screech of his chair and hurried toward the front door.

"Did you know him?" Cace asked. His head held the slightest cant.

Sunny straightened in her chair. "Cary. I work with him. He said he had to go."

"Leaving most of his food?"

Sunny glanced over her shoulder where Cary's tray still sat, a short pile of brisket and a side of potato salad untouched.

Weird. Prosthetists weren't on-call. Maybe he had a personal issue.

"Did y'all save room for cobbler?" Karena appeared table-side carrying a tray with three bowls of peach cobbler, all topped with a generous scoop of vanilla ice cream. "On the house."

"Oh, no, Maj—Karena. We can pay for them." Sunny had already eyed the cobbler while in line. She'd pay double what they wanted if the bowls' contents tasted half as good as the gooey-creamy dessert looked.

Karena laughed. "No way. I know you'll be back. You can pay for one then."

The woman was too good to Sunny.

Cace piled their dishes on the empty dinner tray, allowing for room to enjoy the cobbler. Warm peaches and flakey dough met cold, melty creaminess. Sunny smothered a moan when the delicious creation hit her mouth. "This is the real deal," she said to Karena, who'd taken the fourth chair at the table. "David make this too?"

Karena's smile blew up. "Nope. The baked goods are mine. With Texas's finest ice cream, Blue Bell."

"You and David are a lethal combination. Lethal for my arteries, that is."

"Stop," Karena said, deadpan. "Flattery will get you another serving."

"Then we need to keep those compliments coming," Cace said, tipping an empty bowl toward their benefactress.

"I'll grab another then." She propped her hands on the table to rise.

"No," he said with a laugh and a pat on his abdomen. "I couldn't possibly eat anything else. Are y'all going to be open for lunch?"

"We're closed after three on Sunday and reopen at eleven on Tuesday."

"Great. I'm telling everybody I work with about this place."

Her smile hitched with a grimace. Karena shifted a bit, stretching out her leg with the prothesis.

Sunny tracked the movement. "Overdo it a bit?"

Karena's brows gathered together, and she opened her mouth to say something. She must've thought better of her words because nothing emerged. Then her shoulders dropped a fraction. "A bit."

That she admitted her exhaustion shocked Sunny. She'd expected the proud comeback Karena had been poised to deliver. For several minutes they made small talk, then Garrett joined Cace when he said he wanted to talk to David for a moment since there was a lull in customers.

"Thank you for letting me sit here," Karena said with a tight smile.

"Good grief, lady. You can take a load off for a couple of minutes. Look around you. Your tables are turning over well. People are coming in the door and going through the line quickly. And they are loving your food. You have plenty of people serving the line and bussing the tables. This is going to be successful."

"Yeah, I feel like I'm not doing anything when everyone else has a job. All because of this," she gestured to her leg, where the jeans covered her prosthesis. Someone would've had to look closely to see the steel portion peeking from the hem where the shaft connected to the foot in a tennis shoe.

"I doubt you've done nothing," Sunny continued before Karena could utter her denial. "You did the desserts. I'm sure you helped get the place ready, helped string the bunting and the banner. Probably cleaned every table, every chair, and the bathrooms before you opened today."

"Guilty," David said from behind his wife's chair. His face filled with pride, he set his hands on her shoulders and glanced at Sunny, Cace, and Garrett. "But the most important thing is she's my biggest supporter. When my entire family told me I must be nuts to get out of the Army to start a catering business, she was there, telling me I should follow my dream. You can't hire that. Her support is more valuable than gold." He dipped his face down and shared his loving smile with his wife. "Besides, where am I going to find someone to make the cobbler? It's like crack. I could eat the whole pan."

Karena mock-punched David in the shoulder and favored him with an exaggerated eye-roll.

The humor saved Sunny from the tears threatening to fall. "Y'all are terrible."

"The General here is just worried I'll get along fine without her while she's gone." He patted her shoulder then turned back to return to his cash register.

Ha-ha. He'd promoted his wife to general. Probably a fit title. "Gone?"

Karena turned to Sunny, eagerness lighting her smile. "Ossocorp called yesterday. They want to fly me out to Colorado on Monday so I can get fitted with a blade test model. They think I'll be an excellent subject."

Whoa. Quick. "When did you apply?"

"Last Monday." Every bit of pain she'd exhibited earlier evaporated, replaced by a glow of expectation, like a child at Christmas. "I'm so excited."

The company moved fast. Too quickly? "Did someone from Ossocorp come down and do a physical of you? Look at your medical records?"

"No, I submitted my paperwork. They didn't ask for my records."

A company like Ossocorp, the wonder child of the prosthetic world with their advances in bioelectrical control, wouldn't randomly select someone for their test programs without a physical evaluation or reviewing her records. How would they know where her scars were and how that might interact with the electrodes? Did they know the length of her residual leg? So many questions. But Sunny didn't want to pop Karena's bubble. Maybe this would be a nice trip for her, and she'd mistaken the inquiry for a preliminary evaluation, rather than acceptance into the program.

Cace and Garrett returned, each bearing a refill of tea glasses, including hers. Despite her worries, Sunny lifted her cup. "To Karena. May her new blade take her farther, faster, and stronger to that goal of a marathon next year."

Garrett and Cace raised their glasses with her.

"Okay. So y'all are taking home a whole pan of cobbler tonight," Karena said.

About to comment on the amount of time she'd have to spend on the running trail, a fine vibration in her fingers stole Sunny's attention, like with Ms. Randle. The thumb drive? Her Gift wanted her to give the device to who? Karena? The buzzing increased. Must be a yes.

"Hey, I found a thumb drive on the exam table when I went back to clean up yesterday after our session. It must've fallen from your shorts' pocket." Sunny pulled the device from her purse without looking at her boyfriend, in case he remembered where she'd said she'd found the drive.

Karena accepted the small, plastic rectangle from Sunny. Her face screwed up a bit when she examined what she'd been given, then cleared. "Oh. The thumb drive I had saved the marketing plan on. How did it get in my shorts? Huh." She slipped the device into one of the front pockets of her jeans. "Thanks. There's a bunch of advertising and other things I don't want to have to recreate on this baby. You're a sweetheart."

Sunny wanted to do a happy dance. Two for two and all in a day.

CHAPTER 9

Sunday morning dawned bright. By the emptiness in the bed next to her and the smell of coffee brewing, Cace had already risen. He rarely slept in. Military training died hard.

She joined him on the couch with a steaming mug and curled her legs under her. Having AC again was awesome. She tugged her t-shirt hem back down over her yoga pants. "What's up?"

His brows gathered, and he lifted his gaze from his phone's screen. With a scrub of his hand over his face, he said, "They want me to come in early. At two, if I can."

Belton, like many police departments, had a hard time filling officer vacancies, and Cace often worked extra days or additional hours. He'd already worked one of his days off, yesterday.

"Watch that they don't burn you out." She blew on her coffee before taking a sip, then gauged his reaction over the rim.

"The overtime pay is worth the extra hours."

"Mmm." Her mumbled non-agreement didn't erase the worry. Bad enough to work a forty-hour week and face the unknown. A fifty-hour week added significantly to his risk. She swallowed the worry. He loved what he did. She'd have to trust in what she'd termed his superpower—an uncanny ability to know when things were wrong and to keep her safe. Just like he trusted her not to do anything dangerous, even if her Gift wanted her to. And to make him feel better, she'd enrolled in the Krav Maga classes. Well, taking the self-defense classes had been at his urging. Now, she really liked learning how to protect herself and enjoying how much more confident the martial art made her feel about the world.

"Shoot. We were going to go look for a sofa today." The one they sat on had traveled with her from college through physical therapy school and now here. The beige leather couch, with all the nicks and stains, desperately needed to be replaced.

"We can still go."

She almost laughed at his half-hearted protest. "Most places don't open until noon on a Sunday. Why don't we try next Saturday? That would give us five or six hours to shop."

Something akin to panic flared in his eyes.

Amusement rose within her. "Is big, bad Officer Navarro afraid of five hours of furniture shopping?" She took in his reaction over the cup's rim.

He snorted. "Afraid? No. Terrified? Yes."

A knock at the door cut her giggles short, and her gaze flashed to the clock on the fireplace mantle. Eight on the dot. "Early on a Sunday for people to be up."

"I'll get it." Cace rose from the couch and went to the door. After a quick look through the peephole, he unlocked the blind deadbolt and swung the panel open. "Can I help you?"

The position of his body screened the person standing outside from Sunny's view.

"Is Sunshine Flannigan home?"

She knew that male voice, though nearly a year had passed since he told her the investigation he'd opened on her for allegedly lying on her application had been dropped. The accusation still stung. As did the humiliation of being walked out of the building by Sherry and VA Security.

Sunny uncurled herself and stood, crossing to Cace, who shifted a bit to accommodate her at the door.

Agent Fowler stood outside with a woman. Unlike the last time they'd met, when he'd been in a suit, today he wore khakis and a black polo shirt branded with an embroidered gold badge and 'Veterans Affairs Office of Inspector General' underneath. The woman wore a similar outfit, with a royal blue polo.

Sunny took a sip from her coffee mug to allow herself to tamp down the apprehension spiraling through her. "What can I do for you, Agent Fowler?"

"I apologize for the early morning visit. We were hoping to speak with you."

On a Sunday? At eight in the morning? "About what?" Sunny managed to keep her tone civil.

"Something's happened at the VA, and we need to find out what you know."

Sunny's rule-follower nature warred with the still raw nerve which didn't favor extending them much courtesy. Her upbringing won out. Though not by much. "If y'all wait outside for a couple of minutes, I'll get dressed."

She spun, not waiting for Cace to shut the door in their faces. She grabbed a pair of jeans, and a t-shirt and carried them to the bathroom. The vague, weird paranoia about being watched lingered. How she wished she could shake off Walter. No windows in the bathroom gave her an extra sense of privacy.

Cace joined her, leaning his shoulder against the doorjamb. He'd already donned a pair of jeans. "Are you sure you want to talk to them? And even if you *want* to, are you sure you want to talk to them here without the benefit of representation?"

"I think I'm okay here." She dropped her gaze from his reflection in the mirror and applied toothpaste to her toothbrush. "I learned last time that if they start asking questions, I can say I'm not answering anything else and tell them to leave."

"Well, if they're going to arrest you, you might want to look a little more responsible in front of the judge than jeans and a Country Swing Kings t-shirt."

Her stomach bottomed out. She pulled her toothbrush from her mouth and mumbled around the foam, "You think they're going to arrest me?"

"Poor attempt at humor." He grimaced an apology. "I think they would've snagged you immediately when you came to the door. Cops don't want to give people time to think if there's an arrest warrant out for them. Dressing the part for the meeting is a power move. It gives you confidence and makes them take you more seriously." He turned and his reflection disappeared from the mirror when he entered the walk-in closet. "I'm going to stay with you unless you want me to leave, okay?"

Wear something more responsible? She continued scrubbing with her toothbrush, then spit. A clip held the hair she scraped back into a ponytail.

When she emerged from the bathroom, Cace tucked his shirttail into his jeans. After another trip to the closet, she'd hastily donned a pair of black pants, a floral-patterned blouse, and black flats. Respectability-R-Us.

She reentered the bedroom. "Ready?" she asked him.

He jerked a nod and swept his arm out, indicating she should precede him.

She crossed to the door, her nerves bundled in her gut. After placing her hand on the knob, she paused to take a deep breath and release the calming air. Pasting the biggest smile on her face, she opened the door.

The two agents jumped to their feet from the cafe chairs flanking a small table she'd placed on the wide, covered porch.

"Please, come in." The gracious words carried an undertone of sarcasm, one she didn't feel obligated to strip out. "Let's sit at the table," she added once they'd filed inside. A sofa and a club chair would make for awkward seating.

Sunny snagged her coffee cup from the counter and poured herself a refill. Her gaze swung to the two agents who, like Case, were still standing. "Would you like a cup?" She gestured with the pot.

The two shared a glance. Agent Fowler said "Thank you," at the same time the woman said, "Sure."

Sunny didn't hurry to pull two mugs down and pour the coffee. The simple act of making them wait gave her a sense she had better control of the situation and settled her nerves a bit. "Cream and sugar?"

"No, thank you," the two agents said in unison.

Sunny handed them their mugs across the bar counter, then said, "Cace? A refill?"

Humor danced in his eyes, echoing the shadow of a smile. He knew her tactic. "Sure." At a lazy pace, he crossed to the coffee table and brought his half-empty cup to her.

She poured, then brought the steaming mug to the table. She chose the side. Last time Agent Fowler questioned her, she'd been sandwiched between him and another agent and the pressure made Sunny feel the squeeze play. If they were here for the same purpose, she wouldn't grant them the power.

The agents settled like Sunny wanted, him at the other end of the table opposite Cace, and the woman taking the long stretch.

Sunny assumed her seat across from the female agent.

Fowler opened his portfolio and removed a pen from the holder attached. "I'm sure you're—"

Sunny turned to the woman. "I'm sorry, I didn't get your name?"

"Oh, uh..." the woman reached behind her, brought forward a black wallet, and flipped the halves open, displaying the credentials with a picture which more or less matched. In the photo, she'd chosen to wear a navy suit with a light-blue, button-down blouse and put her auburn hair completely up. Today, she wore a low ponytail. "Special Agent Tilly Brown."

"Nice to meet you." Sunny said and turned to Agent Fowler. "My apologies. I may have interrupted?"

A ghost of a smile hung on the man's lips as if he understood Sunny's strategy. "I was going to say I'm sure you're wondering why we're here."

The female agent laid her credentials on the table and opened the folio she'd brought, retrieved a pen, the click saying she was prepared to write.

Agent Fowler adjusted his glasses. "How long have you worked for the VA?"

"You don't remember? You had me walked off the campus not even a week after I started. Just over a year."

The small smile faltered and disappeared from his face. Maybe antagonizing him wasn't the best idea before she knew his purpose.

"I do remember." He laid his pen carefully on the notepad he'd not written on yet. "I guess I'll cut through the small talk."

"Probably best," Cace said from the other end. "She still hasn't forgiven you for not double-checking her computer file before putting her through the wringer." His tone carried a hard edge, seemingly not inclined to forgive them either. While police officers often gave federal agents support, apparently Cace drew the line at the agent using intimidation to get Sunny to resign when she hadn't done a thing wrong.

A wan smile swept across Agent Fowler's face. "I can understand. I don't know if we could've cleared you without your own investigation into Ben Moody. His computer gave us everything we needed to exonerate you. He was very good, and our computer system is, unfortunately, not the best at detecting hackers."

Probably the best apology she'd get. And he'd been doing his job using the information he had, which sucked. She sighed and dropped the brittle edge. "What's going on that brings you here at eight a.m. on a Sunday. Presumably, agents do get the day off."

The ghost of a smile returned. "We're doing a preliminary inquiry into HIPAA violations involving amputees at Temple's clinic."

The statement hit Sunny like a longhorn stampede. Stealing or releasing patients' medical information was a sure way to get fired and prosecuted. The VA went overboard with the sheer volume of acknowledgements she had to sign during her orientation. And about every piece of paper in a patient's records had a HIPAA warning. No one could say they weren't aware of the penalties for violating the law.

Agent Fowler leaned forward in his chair, and his gaze

lasered in on her. "Have you taken or downloaded or borrowed or used any patient information from the computer or hardcopy files of any type?"

"No." The denial leapt from her lips. "I'd never steal patient information. Ever."

"So, you've not downloaded *any* patient information." One eyebrow popped over the upper rim of his glasses.

"Absolutely not." She shook her head side to side to emphasize her answer.

He shared a glance with Agent Brown before returning his gaze to Sunny. "Would you be surprised if I told you your log-in was used to download patient information?"

CHAPTER 10

It took several seconds for Sunny to regain her breath. Holy cheezus. Someone used her password to steal HIPAA information? But *she* hadn't downloaded anything. Would she lose her job? Go to prison? She stared into her half-full mug sitting on the dining table like the coffee held the answers.

Cace's hand covered hers on the dining table's top. "Maybe now might be a good time to take a break."

She nodded. He thought she should throw the agents out. Not yet. She'd tell the truth. "I didn't do anything wrong. If another person used my login to steal patient information, someone stole my password."

"How could someone steal your password?" Agent Fowler sat back a bit in his chair.

"I don't know. Maybe they looked over my shoulder while I logged on. Or maybe I forgot to log off of the computer." What other ways could there be?

"Okay." He glanced to Agent Brown, who still scribbled on her notepad. He continued when she looked up. "If you didn't steal the information, who did?"

Who in the clinic would do that? Shelly? Brinna?

Cary? Malcolm? Shawna? The receptionists? "I don't know. I can't really see anyone stealing HIPAA information. What kind? Only information on amputees?"

Agent Fowler jerked his chin down along with his spoken, "Yes."

"That doesn't mean only employees of the amputee group could've stolen the data, you know. Anyone with access to a VA computer could." Her mind whirled, her thoughts darting from who to why to how.

He folded his hands over his notebook. "I get that. Can you think of anyone? Has anyone mentioned taking expensive trips, buying a new house maybe?"

To make money? What information could be sold, and who would buy patient information? "No. Nothing out of the ordinary. At least from their behavior since I've been there. How long has this been going on?"

He shared another look with his coworker before responding. "It looks like for about six months."

She squinted and stared out the window while she moved pieces of information around in her head. "Well, that takes Malcolm out. He's only worked there for the last two months. You probably already knew that. And Shawna's due back next week from six weeks of maternity leave. You probably already knew that too. So, if the thefts were happening during that time, I'd have to say Shelly, Brinna, and Cary. At least in the amputee clinic."

"And you," Agent Brown said.

Sunny narrowed her lids and focused on the woman across from her. "I absolutely did not steal information."

"Right." She dipped her head and scribbled more in her notebook.

"Okay," Agent Fowler said, drawing Sunny's attention back to him. "Actually, I tend to believe you. I have to ask the questions though."

A trickle of relief started, but Sunny cut the emotion short. He was doing his job. Didn't mean she had to like it.

"All of the employees' sign-ons have been used to download the information, not only yours," he said.

Whoa. Anger began to build. They targeted her first? "Including Shawna's?"

The agent nodded.

"Good grief. You sounded like you suspected me. You have no idea who committed the thefts?"

"Didn't you say the computer systems were easily hacked?" Cace said, leaning forward in his chair.

Good catch. Sunny shifted her gaze back to the agent, victory surging through her. She didn't do this.

Faint red color rose on Agent Fowler's cheeks. "Yes. However, we don't think we have an outside job, since we believe the downloads were traced to computers in the Physical Therapy wing."

Rats. Still, the pool widened beyond her own work area. "So not just computers used in the amputee section?"

"Right." A fleeting expression, maybe frustration, flitted across his face.

Her mind raced, then lit on another subject. "I thought that place has a surveillance camera system."

"It should." His lips flattened. "Not every camera works. And whoever is stealing the information knows which don't."

Wait. What? The cameras don't all work?

Cace squeezed her hand again. She didn't look at him, understanding his message the time had come to boot the agents out. One last question. "Why steal information solely about amputees? If you're going to steal someone's identity, why wouldn't you take every patient's?"

Agent Brown flipped her notebook shut, seeming to understand the interview was over. "It's what we're looking into. You can use medical information for a variety of reasons, not merely identity theft. Maybe someone wants to market to amputees. Who knows?"

Market only to amputees? That made little sense. What kind of market existed for—

Both of the agents pushed back from the table, their chairs squeaking a bit across the wood floor. Agent Fowler pulled a card from a side pocket before he shut his folder. He proffered the rectangle to Sunny. "If you hear or see or find anything, call me on my mobile."

Sunny palmed the card, then she pushed to her feet and followed them the short distance to the door. Cace prowled on her heels, her silent protector. "I can do that," she said.

Agent Fowler paused, his hand on the doorknob. "I really don't think you stole the information. Though, I can't stress enough that if you did, the time to tell us is now."

Couldn't resist one last attempt, could you? She shook her head negatively, her ponytail brushing against her nape. "I didn't steal anything."

He jerked a slight nod. "I had to at least ask. Like last time, please don't talk about this to anyone else. You two have a good day."

Cace shut the door behind them with a snap, and she flopped on the couch, covering her face with her hands. Her bottom met the most worn area right over a support. *Ouch.* She rubbed her offended tailbone. "Dang, we need to get a new sofa. And I apparently need to get a new job. That's twice in one year these people have accused me of committing a crime." She'd attempted a joking tone, but ended on a sob.

Cace eased into the arm chair which sat perpendicular

to the couch and leaned his elbows on his knees. "You okay?"

"Yeah. I...I..." Frustration overwhelmed her. "Why does this keep happening to me?" she wailed, dashing at her eyes when the tears fell.

He shifted to the couch and took her into his arms, smoothing her back, while she cried out her emotions. The fury, the frustration, the fear. Finally, she got a hold of her tears. She hitched a breath and pushed back a bit. How she hated breaking down. She pulled a tissue from the box on the side table and dabbed at her swollen eyes, blood-shot, too, no doubt. A blow of her nose added to what had to be a lovely picture.

She wadded the scrap of soft paper in her hand. "Sorry about that. I don't know why I cried. I'm so mad right now I don't know what to say." The rage and anxiety rose again, bringing tears to her eyes once more. She ruthlessly pushed them back.

"I understand. First, let's focus on a couple of things. One. It's okay to cry. You've had a stressful couple of days. Walter, then this? Anybody would be crying right now."

She'd forgotten about Walter. A fresh round of fury hit her. No wonder she'd turned into a bundle of nerves.

"Second. You still have a job, which means they don't have anything solid against you. You're one of many suspects." He clasped her hand, the one without the wet tissue, and squeezed slightly. "I did believe Fowler when he said he didn't think you stole the information. Investigators typically don't tell suspects they believe them if they really suspect they committed the crime."

"I hadn't thought about that." She took a deep breath through her mouth, counted to ten, then exhaled. Better. She pecked a kiss on his cheek then fitted her nose and forehead to his to stare deep into his eyes. “Thanks for having my back.”

“Thank you for letting me.” His tone dropped to a rumble. “I can think of better ways to spend my Sunday than shopping for a couch. You want a sample?”

She wound her arms around his neck. “Please.” He had the most marvelous way of making her forget her worries.

CHAPTER 11

Sunny reviewed the grocery list in front of her, wracking her brain to make sure she'd remembered everything. She loved shopping at antique malls and for clothing. The weekly food run? Not so much.

"Are you sure you want to go? I can go to the store tomorrow before work if you give me a list." Cace clicked the buckle of his duty belt together and inserted his pistol in the holster. She took him in, all crisp dark navy uniform and hair still damp from the shower.

"I've got it," she said. "I've got a free afternoon. I may hit Chatham's Furniture, though. I'll take pictures if I see a sofa I like."

He dropped a kiss on the top of her head. "See you when I get back. And remember to lock up behind me."

"Be careful," she said right before the door closed. She didn't get the luxury to remind him most days since she was already at work.

She grabbed her purse and her list and headed for the door. Time to shop for a new sofa. Yay. Then her steps slowed. Dang. Now she would become all paranoid about the locks. She peeked around the bedroom doorjamb. Both windows locked. Check. The three windows in the living area locked. Check. Two windows in the dining area. Check. Window over the sink. Check. Now she could leave.

Her phone rang while she threw the bolt on her front door's new lockset. She pulled the device from her purse and tapped the answer button. "Hello?"

"Hi, Sunny? This is Karena."

"Hi Maj—Karena. What can I do for you?" Sunny unlocked her truck, slid up into the driver's seat, and shut the door.

"I don't think this thumb drive is mine. I went to go check something on our marketing plan. Instead, I found what looked like hospital patient information. My drive was in my desk drawer. They look the same, but the one you gave me isn't mine."

Sunny's mouth dried. 'Patient information.' What...? How...? She took a deep breath and forced a swallow. "Okay. I'm out running errands. If you like, I can swing by and get it. Where are you?" She reversed from the gravel lot.

"I'm at the restaurant until four. Or I can drop it off if that works better."

Sunny turned left at the stop sign, a path which would take her toward Temple and Ranger Barbecue. "I'm already out. I'll be by in about ten minutes, if that's okay?"

"See you soon."

Sunny put her phone back into her purse. Why would the Gift have directed her give the drive to Karena if the device didn't belong to her? And how would she explain this to the major? To Cace? Her stomach cramped. To Agent Fowler?

The question rolled around in her mind. Movement in her review mirror dragged her from her thoughts. A dark van tailgated her truck. 'Fiber Now Cable' splashed in orange across the hood, the windows too tinted for her to see the driver. She examined her speedometer. Ugh. Well under the speed limit. She pressed the gas to increase her speed, and the van dropped back. *Pay attention to your driving, woman.*

When she pulled into the parking area, only a couple of spots were open. Good for the Moseleys. They deserved success.

Karena greeted her right inside the doors. "Hey, lady. You're fast." A slight frown gathered, and she scanned over her shoulder before turning back to Sunny. "Come into the office, for a minute?"

"Uh, sure." Maybe the major hadn't told her husband? Sunny followed the other woman down the narrow hallway past the bathrooms to a door with a sign which read, 'No Admittance.'

"What's going on?" Sunny asked once she'd settled into the one side chair in the small, neat office.

Karena swiveled a bit in her black padded office chair in front of the desk. "I would've told you on the phone," she shrugged slightly. "David stepped near, and he gets a little protective over me still."

"I can imagine," Sunny said dryly. The comment hit close to home for her too. She could almost hear what Cace would say when she told him about this.

"As I was getting ready to pull out the thumb drive, I saw my name on a folder. I clicked on the icon." Karena folded her arms. "It has my entire file, from my injury through last week."

Fear gripped Sunny's guts. Oh no. She had to tell Karena. "I'm concerned because I got a visit from VA's OIG this morning."

Karena quirked a brow. "On a Sunday?"

"I know, right? I'm thinking this must be more important than your run-of-the-mill investigation for them to come out on a weekend. They told me someone's been stealing information from the clinic—specifically the amputee patients."

"Which I am."

How could the woman stay so calm when Sunny's knee wanted to bounce a mile a minute? "Yep. They couldn't—or wouldn't—say why they thought someone would steal the information. Full disclosure, I'm on the list of possible suspects."

"Not you." Karena *harrumphed*. "Anyone can tell you're as honest as the day is long."

The major's pronouncement settled uncomfortably on Sunny. She'd lied about how she found the device. But if she told the truth, she'd have to reveal her Gift. What the major had gone through—near death, and a permanently altered life for her country—wiped away Sunny's doubts.

She took a deep breath, then said, "I have a confession. I'm not always honest."

"What do you mean?" A bit of steel had entered the major's tone.

"I didn't find the drive on the exam table. I found it in the parking lot."

Karena cocked her head. "Then why in the world would you say you did and give the thing to me?"

"It's not something I tell everyone. I have a…strange family." Suddenly, admitting her psychic gift seemed a bad idea.

"Don't we all?" The major snort-laughed.

Too late to stop now. Sunny laced her fidgety fingers together in her lap. "My eldest sister sees and can talk to ghosts. My youngest sister has psychic visions."

That quieted the major's chuckles. "And you?"

"I…I *find* things." Her hands flew apart, then fluttered a bit with her insecurity. Karena probably thought her a kook. Sunny rushed on, saying, "Then I give them to the people who are supposed to have them. Like the thumb drive."

"So, I was supposed to have this thumb drive?" Karena's words came slowly, with a squinched-up nose.

"I think so. My Gift told me."

"Your *Gift*?" She could've used derision. Instead, her tone spoke of curiosity.

The smallest bit of tension seeped from Sunny's shoulders. "It's an old family term. A shortened version of The Flannigan Gift. Supposedly, we descend from a long line of Irish mystics, women who had the Sight. We weren't aware there were other aspects to the power, such as seeing ghosts or whatever you'd call mine."

Karena took a moment, maybe digesting the information, maybe trying to figure out if she should call 9-1-1 and get Sunny a psych eval. Finally, she said, "Why did you lie to me?"

"Would you have taken the flash drive if I told you this story?"

Another pause. "Okay. What do I do, then? I don't want these people's personal and medical information."

Sunny considered the plan she'd formed while she drove over. The Gift didn't direct her, so giving the drive to law enforcement must be okay. "Do you mind if I call the agent? I told him if I found anything I would let him know. Since they were here this morning, they still might be around this afternoon."

"I'd prefer David not know about this."

The comment stopped Sunny's quest for her phone. "The patient information or my gift? You two okay?"

She grimaced. "Sure. I overdid it a bit yesterday, and we had a little argument last night. I know he means well."

"Yeah. Been there with my guy." So far, the truce between she and Cace had held. He didn't go all overprotective, plus, she took her self-defense classes and carried her mace on her keychain. "Out of curiosity, you didn't seem weirded-out when I told you about my Gift."

The major gave her a rueful smile. "I grew up in Charleston, South Carolina, but my family comes from a tiny community on the coast, in the Low Country. Though they both wanted to forget where they came from, I always enjoyed the time I spent with my grandparents. There's a strong belief in the supernatural in those communities. Granny always brought the root doctor to the house to bless me before my parents came to pick me up. She said the practice kept away the 'haunts'—the evil spirits. I like to think she protected me." Her eyes had grown distant while she spoke, then refocused and landed on Sunny. "So, magic or the paranormal isn't hard for me to believe."

A little bubble of joy grew in Sunny's heart. The major didn't think her a freak. "Someday I'd love to hear more about your family."

"It seemed almost magical back then," she said with a misty smile before sobering. "Isn't most of childhood?"

"True." Sunny had been five when her parents were killed by a drunk driver, and she'd grown up in a tiny town, in a giant house, raised by a clairvoyant grandmother. A little sad, but a little magical too.

A knock on the door heralded a young woman, one of the restaurant employees, Sunny guessed, based on the Ranger Barbecue t-shirt she wore. "Hey, Mrs. Moseley. I'm having trouble closing out one of the registers. Darn thing keeps giving me an error. Can you help me?"

"Be right there," Karena said, and the teen shut the door. She pushed to her feet with a slight wince.

Concern filled Sunny. "Don't overdo."

Karena huffed a breath. "Yeah, I don't want to mess up my opportunity with Ossocorp. The meeting's tomorrow, and my flight's out of Austin at seven tonight." She handed the thumb drive to Sunny. "I'm sure the OIG agents might want to talk to me. Let them know I should be back on Wednesday. You can give them my phone number."

Sunny stood and put the drive in her shorts pocket. Hopefully she hadn't irrevocably damaged their friendship. "Thanks. I'm sorry for involving you in this. And I'm sorry for lying to you. It won't happen again."

"It's not the worst lie I've ever been told and not going to be the last. Thank you for your honesty."

"Thank you for believing in me." The woman had a good ten years on Sunny, but she felt as if they were becoming friends. "Good luck tomorrow," she said to Karena and waved at David. He stood behind the counter, still busy with patrons at two in the afternoon.

Sunny fished for her phone on the way to the truck and found the card she'd stashed in her wallet. After a couple of quick taps on the screen, she put the phone to her ear, then switched on the ignition to start the cool air from the vents. While she waited for the agent to answer, she wished for an early arrival of a cold front forecasted for Wednesday. Highs in the fifties meant she could break out her sweaters.

She'd almost given up when he answered. "This is Agent Fowler."

The formal tone caught her off-guard and her nerves began a two-step in her stomach. "Hi, uh, this is Sunny—

Sunshine Flannigan. I think I may have something for you."

He paused long enough for her to think maybe the call had dropped. "Can we meet you at the north side employee entrance at the VA Hospital in ten minutes?"

"Sure." Sunny backed out of her spot, then turned onto the street, a load of questions bouncing around in her mind. Why did the Gift have her give the drive to Karena? The silly paranormal power obviously didn't mind her giving it to the agents or she would be experiencing its displeasure, tingles, pushes, something. Was Karena supposed to have seen she'd been victimized? She reviewed the table talk from the previous night. Surely not that. The only bit Sunny learned had been the news Karena had been accepted for the Ossocorp program.

Except the Major hadn't been evaluated yet.

Ding ding ding ding.

The sound echoed through her brain. Ossocorp hadn't *evaluated* her yet.

Ding ding ding ding.

So, if she'd been accepted into the program without a prior evaluation, that would mean…

They already had her file.

Ding ding ding ding.

Holy crap. Someone stole the information for Ossocorp, the rising darling of the prosthetic world. The company would get a head start on all the evaluations, would have a patient database at their fingertips, all with good government insurance.

More dinging.

A honk behind her let her know the light had been green for a moment. She shook her head to clear her shock and proceeded through the intersection. A Fiber Now van pulled in behind her, like the one which followed her to the restaurant. Wait. Didn't Walter work for that company?

She searched the rearview mirror for any clue of who drove the van. The sunshade had been pushed down, obscuring the driver's face. She mashed the accelerator, and her truck jumped forward. Another glance in her mirror showed the van had dropped back a bit.

Calm down. Fiber Now's vehicles were everywhere. They'd moved into the market a couple of months ago, trying to take over from the more established companies. Right? Right.

The van reappeared at her tailgate, obliterating the pep-talk.

She accelerated.

The van accelerated.

She moved into a left-hand turn lane.

The van moved into the left-hand turn lane.

Her heart rate kicked up to near explosion.

The light gave her an arrow to turn across traffic. She made the turn, closely followed by the van, orange letters bright against the black hood.

Cheese and crackers. *Stay calm. You're going to meet with federal agents. You'll be okay. They'll know what—*

The van turned right and fell away from sight.

She passed a shaky hand over her face. She needed to get a grip. No one was out to get her.

CHAPTER 12

Agents Fowler and Brown waited at the door for Sunny when she arrived, her heartbeat and breathing back under control after her massive bout with paranoia. A glass of wine wouldn't be out of order with dinner tonight. Though first, she had to figure out a way to not be a suspect.

The agents escorted her to a conference room, the same room in which she'd met Agent Fowler almost a year ago. The coincidence caused nerves to dance in her belly.

Once she entered, she immediately took a seat at the end of the long side of the table, not wanting to be sandwiched between the two. Strategic. There was a good possibility they might not buy her explanation of how she came by the thumb drive.

The agents settled themselves, with Agent Fowler at the head and Agent Brown across from her. As she had this morning, Agent Brown opened her portfolio and started to write, even before Sunny said a word.

"Thank you for calling us." Eagerness shaded his tone. "You said you found something?"

She pulled the thumb drive from her shorts pocket and

pushed it to him. "I found this in the parking lot Friday evening when I left. I thought it belonged to a friend, so I gave it to her. She said she accessed the files and found patient information. She gave it back to me right before I called you."

Stunned could be the only word for the expression on both the agents' faces.

He recovered first. "Where did you find this?"

"In the parking lot." *Didn't I just say that?*

"*Where* in the parking lot?"

"You know those planting areas throughout the parking area? If you look out the employee door, there's one of those to the right. The thumb drive was between the next two spaces, before you get to the planting area on the second row."

"Okay. Who did you give it to?"

Idiot. Karena would have a different story than her. If she were going to lie, Sunny should've coordinated with Karena beforehand to make her version more plausible. Besides, feeding the federal agents a bogus story wouldn't make them believe her more if they ferreted out the truth. Doubtful their reaction would match Karena's.

Her shoulders tensed for the looks of pity or disbelief or derision. "I have this weird internal thing where I find objects. Then I give them to who's supposed to have them."

Agent Fowler's face smoothed to a careful neutral. "You find things then give them to the person who's supposed to have them." The scratches of Agent Brown's pen on paper grew loud in his pause. "How do you know who that person is?"

Probably not going to believe her. Yay. She started and needed to finish. "Here's where I may start sounding weird." She continued through the suspicion in the agents' expressions. “The same sense that has me find stuff, also tells me who to give it to.”

The pen scratching stopped, and the two agents shared a glance. For sure both didn’t believe her. Great. Though now she’d told the truth, she wouldn’t have to remember a sequence of events she made up. “I know this sounds weird. That’s what the Gift does.”

“The Gift?” Agent Fowler asked.

“The family story is I have an ancestor who allegedly fled with her family from Ireland to avoid getting burned at the stake in the early seventeen hundreds. Supposedly, she had what the Irish call the Sight—psychic visions—plus she practiced herbcraft. The witch-burners here in colonial America didn’t like her either. She sacrificed herself so her husband and children could escape. The power has descended down the female line since then. My younger sister has the full-on Flannigan Gift, like the family says, the visions and stuff. Me? I have this weird thing.” She shrugged.

Agent Fowler nodded. “So, this…Gift…told you to give the thumb drive to me?”

Skeptical, yet not outright scoffing. His reaction could’ve been worse. “No and yes. I was told to give it to Major Karena Moseley. She’s one of my patients from the clinic. Or used to be.”

“Why would you give the drive to her?”

“Well, the Gift said to.” She continued with her explanation, despite her own concern about the Gift’s purposes. “I don’t know why for sure. It doesn’t tell me things, just lets me know with physical sensations what to do. Anyway, I think the Gift wanted me to find out the drive’s contents.”

“You didn’t look earlier to tell you who to give it to?” Agent Fowler drummed his fingers, their rapping an emphasis to his impatient tone.

Now *that* she had a good answer for. "No. Someone could've had private stuff on there. Plus there could've been viruses on it, and I don't want to have to get a new computer."

"Makes sense," Agent Brown said under her breath. Maybe she believed Sunny.

"So, you gave the drive to Major Moseley." Agent Fowler said. "Why would she access the files if *you* didn't?"

A little more confident, Sunny said, "She has a similar one. I saw her on Friday and told her she must've dropped it at the clinic."

"But you found the drive in the employee lot?" He sat back in his chair and crossed his arms.

Sunny leaned her elbows on the table. "I told her the truth today. She believes me, by the way."

"You lied to her." The skepticism returned in his tone full-force.

Ugh. Can't he see she told the truth now? Whoa. Maybe the Gift was keeping her safe by ensuring she didn't access the files.

Ding, ding, ding.

She shook off her wonder and countered the agent's statement. "The most important thing is I found out what was on the drive. Entire patient files. She said maybe fifty total."

The skepticism dropped from his features, and he sat forward in his chair. "Hers?"

"You said earlier there could be any reason for the theft. What if a company wanted to use those files to find potential patients for treatment by skipping a step?"

He blinked at her behind his wire-rimmed glasses.

Sunny took his lack of comment as encouragement to continue with her theory. "After I gave Karena the drive last night, she said Ossocorp had admitted her into a program for new trials. She's flying out tonight to Ossocorp for a meeting tomorrow. I specifically asked if the company wanted to see her to evaluate her for the program—they're doing a lot of experimental stuff with prostheses and—"

"We're familiar with Ossocorp."

Interesting hard edge to his tone. "Oh. Okay," Sunny said. "Well, Karena told me they contacted her out of the blue a couple of days ago and advised her she had been admitted into their program. No physical evaluation. They didn't discuss what type of amputation she had. Merely admitted." Sunny poked her index finger on the table's surface. "How could they afford to randomly admit amputees into a specialized program like that? Only if they hand-picked them from records they already had. Karena said she didn't give them a copy of her file."

He picked up the thumb drive. "Fifty amputees are on this?"

"Roughly. Karena told me that. I still haven't accessed the files."

"So, if we do a forensic review of this drive, we're not going to see anyone accessed this between Friday night when you found it and now."

"Except for Karena."

"Do you have a computer?"

"Yes. A laptop."

"Then we will have to image your computer to make sure you're telling the truth."

For the love of chicken-fried steak. If they wouldn't take her word, they'd have to find evidence. Nothing would be on her laptop. "I rarely use my computer. I really use my phone most."

"We'll also need to image that too." He turned to Agent Brown. "Did you bring the Cellibrite?" With her nod, he shifted back to Sunny. "We can do that here, right now."

What was a Cellibrite? "Why would you want to see my phone?"

"If you primarily use it for emails and calls, I'll need to verify you haven't been communicating with anyone about the HIPAA information on this. The system will copy the data we need." He tapped the drive. "And your computer for the same reason."

No. Though she had nothing outrageous on her phone, no naked photos or anything like that, no phone copying, no computer copying.

"Ms. Flannigan. I know you feel we're being invasive. Please remember, you brought this to us. With what many would consider a crazy story. If you're not the one who stole the patient information, how am I supposed to verify that? Assuming you aren't the thief, when we do catch who did this, and when I send the case to the U.S. Attorney, they're going to want to know if I verified your statements, because that's what the defense would attack."

Her breath hitched.

She hadn't considered how the version of events would look in court. Knowing someone didn't believe you was one thing. Though she didn't broadcast her Gift, she'd met plenty of skeptics in her time and had grown used to the derision and disbelief. What would a defense attorney do to her?

It's not like she could back down now. She'd given them the drive and had to pay the price for her stupidity. She should've talked this over with Cace first. Goodness only knew what he'd say when she told him.

With a vague nausea, she reached in her purse, pulled out her phone, and laid it on the table between her and Agent Fowler.

From her portfolio, Agent Brown pulled a piece of paper and began writing. Nerves continued to crawl in Sunny's belly while the silence lengthened. Finally, the other woman slid the paper across the table. "Please sign on the line next to the 'x.'"

'Consent to Search' stretched across the center of the page. With a sick taste in her mouth, Sunny signed on the line and slid the document back.

Agent Fowler collected the form and Sunny's phone then set them to the side. He folded his hands on the table. "We can download the phone now, and we can go with you to get your computer, or one of us can follow you back to your house to pick up the computer while your phone downloads. I'm going to have to send the laptop to the lab to do the image. Our computer forensic guy is pretty good. I can have the computer back to you probably by Wednesday."

"I'll wait for my phone to be downloaded, thank you." Them coming to the apartment would save her an accusation of tampering with evidence.

Agent Brown handed a key fob to her coworker. "The Cellibrite is in my trunk, on the left in the black evidence box."

Evidence. Sunny's phone would be evidence. The nerves zoomed around when he exited the room.

"It's going to be okay, you know." Agent Brown said. "If you didn't do anything wrong, there's no need to worry, right?"

The words brought Sunny little comfort. "Tell that to the people who've been charged with murder and exonerated after years in prison."

CHAPTER 13

It took more than an hour to image Sunny's phone. During the waiting period, Agent Brown tried to make small talk, but eventually the topics petered out because Sunny was too busy mentally berating herself. She should've thought this out better, rather than jumping on her instinct to help the agents.

When he returned her phone, Agent Fowler asked, "Do you still want us to follow you over to your residence?"

Sunny jerked a nod, shoved away from the conference table, and stood. Rip the bandage, right?

The mental posterior chewing continued all the way to her home. By the time she reached the Victorian, she'd worked her emotions into a fine fury, all with one target—herself. She slammed the truck's door harder than necessary, the violent action not lessening her frustration one bit.

The agents parked next to her, exiting their black SUV to join her at the start of the paver track leading to her door.

"Come on. Let's get this over with." The surly tone didn't jive with her usual bright disposition, but she didn't have the will to appear gracious right now.

The two followed her to the porch. "It's in my bedroom," she told them while directing her key to the lock.

"Wait." Agent Brown's sharp word caused Sunny to pause and she followed his pointed finger.

A gap, maybe a quarter of an inch, lay between the door and the jamb, the wood splintered where a tool of some sort forced access. Her insides froze, and she took a step back, her hand at her throat. What if Walter lay in wait for her inside? "No," she choked out in a bare whisper.

"You locked it?"

Fear clogged Sunny's throat, allowing her only to nod, then give a second nod when one of them asked if they could open the door.

Agent Brown used her foot against the bottom of the door and shoved.

It banged against the stopper, making Sunny jump and take another step back.

Inside…chaos. The couch cushions and pillows awry. Knick-knacks on the floor. Books from her shelf strewn among picture frames with smashed glass. That was what she could see from her vantage point. No telling what else the vandal ruined in the rest of the apartment.

Tears gathered in her eyes, and she mercilessly squashed them. Not in front of the agents.

"Your housekeeping skills seemed better when we visited this morning," Agent Fowler said. "Would you like us to make sure no one's in the apartment?"

She nodded, and the two agents drew their weapons. "Police, come out with your hands up," he said, then the two crossed the threshold.

Sunny put her back against the side of the house to keep herself upright, otherwise her shaking knees might give out. She pressed her nails into the paint-covered wood siding. Her fear had morphed to fury. She had no doubt who did this, but zero proof. *Unless he'd left fingerprints.* She'd have to call the police. Federal agents wouldn't have any jurisdiction in a home burglary or stalking investigation. Ugh. Cace would know. May even get the call. How would she keep this from him anyway? Ha. Like he wouldn't notice when he got home.

"Miss Flannigan?" Agent Brown's head poked out from the opening into the apartment. "No one's inside. I need to warn you, whoever did this was very destructive."

Sunny hefted a big breath and let the air out slowly. Of course Walter got ugly. "Right. I had a break in last year." When the agent moved aside, Sunny entered.

Her feet stopped only a few paces inside while she took in her apartment. The other woman hadn't been kidding. When Ben broke in last year, he'd been looking for something in particular, the West Point ring his mother stole. Things had been broken, drawers emptied onto the wood floors, cushions displaced. Today, a stampeding herd of cattle would've done less damage. Nothing remained on the shelves, on the mantle. The television had been yanked from the wall and been given a seemingly full-on, heavy-metal-guitar smashing. From her position, she could see the edge of the kitchen and a couple of overhead cabinets. All open, nothing remained inside, crockery and glass shards littered the floor. Empty holes yawed where drawers had once been. And the odor of bleach permeated the space.

"Are you okay?" The female agent's no-nonsense demeanor turned to pity.

"Okay?" Sunny screeched. She took a moment to get her breathing and heart rate back under control so she could talk like a human and not a scorched cat. "Of course, I'm not okay. Someone destroyed most of my possessions." She didn't even want to go into her bedroom.

"Do you prefer I call 9-1-1, or do you want the pleasure?"

"I'll do it," Sunny said through clenched teeth. "Did you want me to get the computer?"

"Not a good idea to remove something from a crime scene," Agent Brown said. "Besides, I think we should wait with you for safety. Let's go back outside."

Not like Cace wouldn't be here in a flash anyway. He'd probably hear the incident on the radio.

Sunny pulled her phone from her purse and made the call. She stabbed at the red button on her phone's screen once she'd related the information. Less than thirty seconds later, her mobile rang. She didn't need caller ID or her Gift to know who was on the other end.

"What the hell is going on, Sunny? I just saw on my terminal that we had a break-in?" Worry edged his words.

Better than anger. "It's bad. I'm okay though."

He paused for a moment. "I'm headed your way." The line disconnected.

She'd hoped to discuss the matter of the agents with him when he got home, maybe figuring a way to soften the blow about turning over the thumb drive beforehand. She should've known better than to trust her luck. Not only would he probably not be happy with her decision, but also have to process the destruction of their possessions. And he'd balked at shopping for a couch. The random thought made her snort with a laugh which carried an edge of her despair.

"Funny?" Agent Brown asked.

Sunny sighed. "More a silly thought. We were going to look for a new couch and he seemed a bit allergic to furniture shopping. I think we're going to have to shop for more than a sofa."

Agent Brown huffed a laugh, while her male coworker winced and muttered, "Oh yeah."

Tires screeched at the front of the residence. Several seconds later, a tall African American uniformed officer rounded the side of the Victorian. The metal nameplate pinned to his chest said K. Bynam. He must've used his investigative powers to determine Sunny was the one not wearing a badge, a gun, and a VA Office of Inspector General polo shirt.

"Are you okay, ma'am?" Officer Bynam asked. When Sunny nodded, he said, "I think Navarro is on his way."

"Thanks. It's pretty bad in there. Is there any way we can get fingerprints?" Maybe they could nail Walter.

The officer stuck his head in the doorway, then turned back to her. "Maybe. I'll call for a tech." He spoke into the microphone clipped at his shoulder. Sunny introduced the two agents, who mercifully remained mum on why they were there, then Bynam recorded her information in a small notebook he'd pulled from his breast pocket. While he finished, two police cars rolled to a stop in the alley, blocking Sunny's truck and the agents' SUV.

Cace stepped out of the first marked unit, face as dark as a Texas thunderhead, and started down the paver walkway, the female officer from the second unit hot on his heels.

His face smoothed when he stopped at Sunny and held her at arm's length. "Are you okay?"

"I'm okay. I was out." She took a deep breath. "No. I'm not really okay. I'm furious."

He wrapped her in a giant hug. "Me too."

"I'm thinking Walter," she said, resting her cheek against the dark navy polyester of his uniform.

"He was my first thought." He stiffened. "What are *they* doing here?"

She didn't look up because she really didn't want to talk about their presence right now. "I brought them."

"We need to talk." Cace disengaged, then announced to the two officers and two agents who had banded together to form a loose knot, "We're going to the gazebo." He didn't wait for an acknowledgement and steered her in the direction of the small, heavily ginger-breaded structure in the corner of the yard. The shade of the ancient live oak ensured the temperatures would be moderate out of the afternoon sun. Mosquitos, on the other hand, would be fierce. *Stay focused.*

He joined her on the planking which formed a bench along the inside perimeter, enfolding her hands in his. "What happened?"

No censure, no judgement, just sincere worry for her. She'd rather he yell or something, which he'd never done. She related the sequence of events which led from Karena giving her back the thumb drive to discovering the apartment had been trashed.

He fell silent after she finished. Great. She stiffened her spine in anticipation of the lecture to come.

"I do wish you would've called me before you gave them the thumb drive. Maybe we could've mailed it in anonymously or something."

"I should've called you. Too late by the time I realized my mistake. About the mailing, first, I didn't know if giving them the drive was the right thing to do. And two, they might've been able to tell who accessed the files, and Karena would've led them to me anyway. Then I would've had to explain why I wasn't forthcoming."

He shoved his hand through his hair, then nodded his

head. "Honesty is always best. I hate that people might think you're lying."

"Karena doesn't think so. So at least she's in my corner."

"At least someone is." He sat back and rubbed his neck with a hand.

That stopped her cold. "You still are. Right?"

His gaze snapped to hers. "Of course I am. I'm sorry. This Walter thing has me wound a bit."

"Navarro. Crime scene is here," the female officer yelled from across the yard.

"Coming." He stood. "They'll want us to do a walk-through to identify potential places he may have touched and things that were stolen."

"Like they did last year." Sunny's heart cramped. From the doorway, she could tell this would be way worse than the prior break-in.

A muscle jumped in his cheek. "Yeah. Like they did last year."

She and Cace joined the crime scene technician, a female in dark tactical pants and a Belton Police polo identifying her as B. Perez. She came for the prior burglary and hadn't been able to find any usable prints. Sunny's confidence they might be able to nail Walter with forensic evidence plummeted. No. The poor tech couldn't find what wasn't there. Hopefully, Walter left something behind.

When Cace stepped inside, he drew a sharp breath. While Sunny had already experienced the havoc of the ransacked apartment, the wanton destruction and the bleach scent punched her in the gut again.

Perez blew a low whistle. "Man. Someone hates you. They usually steal a flat-screen, not bash something that nice into a million pieces."

The comment added fuel to Sunny's anger.

The forensic tech turned to scan the door. "I'll cast for tool marks."

A step into the bedroom sucked the breath from Sunny's lungs. Giant rips in the mattress. The contents of the dresser dumped on the floor, then the drawers smashed into pieces. In the bathroom, toiletries doused the walls. The scent of bleach grew nearly overwhelming.

"Let me get that," Perez said when Sunny reached for the closet's door handle. "I've got gloves on." She depressed the lever and swung the door open. The chemical odor rolled out in a wave.

Sunny stepped back involuntarily. Every bit of clothing, both hers and Cace's, had been thrown on the floor and doused with bleach, no doubt taken from her own laundry closet. She didn't think she could be more furious, but her blood pressure had to be spiking right now. If only she'd been home. She'd have shown Walter not to mess with her.

"Jeez. This guy *really* doesn't like you two," Perez said.

The gender caught Sunny's curiosity, though she had no doubt who lay behind this mayhem. "Why do you say guy?"

"It would take a bit of strength to rip that television bracket from the wall. Lotta rage in him."

Rage. Sunny took in the destruction and revised her opinion. Maybe best she hadn't been home.

She and Cace retreated to the cafe chairs outside the front door while Perez worked inside. He held Sunny's hand atop the narrow, round table. Though neither she nor he had much to say aloud, she stewed, envisioning everything she'd like to do to Walter Randle.

Bynam stayed with them, while the other female officer who'd arrived earlier left for another emergency call. The two agents said they'd wait in their SUV for Sunny's computer.

"Hey, Bynam, come look at this," Perez said from the doorway.

The officer entered the apartment. Muted conversation drifted from inside, not loud enough Sunny could pick out words.

Bynam reappeared about a minute later. "Can I talk to you for a minute, Navarro?"

Cace looked at her, then back to the other officer. He rose and followed the man to the front corner of the porch.

What was going on? She gained her feet and propped her shoulder against one of the columns at the porch's edge. From this distance she couldn't read their lips, no matter how hard she studied the two men. Must be bad though. Cace appeared ready to snap a steel I-beam in two. Behind them, one of the black, white, and orange Fiber-Now trucks sped by, far exceeding the allowable thirty miles per hour speed limit.

She stared at the service vehicle as it passed, trying to discern if Walter drove the truck. No dice. Too fast.

The men returned to where she leaned. Cace's mouth twisted with his anger and patches of red rode high on his cheekbones. "We have a problem."

Her stomach cramped. "Beyond the break-in?"

"Someone put two wireless cameras in our air conditioning vents. One in the living room, the other in the bedroom."

CHAPTER 14

"Cameras," Sunny said slowly. Her brain had slowed, almost refusing to process his words.

Cace's nostrils flared. "Wireless cameras."

Though she'd largely changed in the bathroom because of what she believed to be unjustified paranoia, she and Cace had made love this morning. In their bed. Rage slammed into her, burning white-hot through her veins. She pushed away from the porch column and planted her fists on her hips. The ugliest oath she'd ever heard Cace utter came from her own mouth. "No wonder I felt like someone watched me the past couple of days."

"I thought I was being paranoid," Cace said through tight lips.

"Perez found them," Bynam said. "Saw a glint in the grate and climbed up to investigate. We're hoping to get prints from the cameras, and hopefully the detectives will be able to get a serial number. It's impossible to know exactly how long they've been up there, but the lack of dust suggests not long."

Not long. Like two days or less? Her brain had

unfrozen and began to work overtime, picturing Walter climbing up onto her furniture to reach the grates. He could be the only suspect. Who else had access to their apartment?

Cace told Bynam about the interaction with Walter, along with the man's criminal history.

The officer shook his head, sunlight glinting of his bald scalp.

Heat continued to bubble in her blood. Wait. She may have just seen him fleeing.

"He works for Fiber-Now Cable. I saw one of their trucks sprinting down the street while y'all were talking." Surely, Walter was trying to figure out how to get his cameras out.

The officer scratched his cheek. "I don't know the signal range for those things. Could be blocks, could be a hundred yards, could be fifty feet."

Perez emerged from the door holding two clear plastic bags containing black electronic equipment and several paper bags. Her camera hung from a lanyard strapped to her wrist, and a dark smudge marked her cheek. "I think that's all. I have plenty of identifiable prints. Their placement, on doors, the lock, and other common surfaces means you and Cace are going to have to come down to the office and give a set of prints. I'm out of elimination cards right now for some reason. There were also small scrapes along the face of the lock plate, so I took a cast for tool marks, along with the jamb and door. My guess? A small crowbar, one of those foot-long models." A wan, lopsided smile appeared on the woman's face. "I don't think you're going to want to stay there tonight. The bleach smell is still strong. And I spread powder over God and everything in there, like last time."

A car door slammed behind Sunny, and she turned to see Agent Fowler approaching down the paver walkway. *Not now. No. Now. Get him off your back so you can lick your wounds in private.*

"Did you happen to see my laptop while you were in there?" she asked Perez.

"Nope. Didn't see a laptop."

No laptop? Concern heaped on top of her still-simmering fury. "Can I go in?"

"Yep. I'm done."

Sunny entered the apartment and made a beeline for the bedroom, where she'd left her computer a couple of days ago. Though Perez must've shut the closet door, the bleach smell permeated the room and made Sunny's eyes water. She poked around the clothing, the jumble of bedding, looked under the bed, behind the nightstands. No laptop. Not in the bathroom either. She opened the closet door and the wave of bleach hit her again, though not as strong.

"What are you doing?" Cace asked from behind her.

"The VA agents want my laptop. I can't find it in here. Maybe he threw it in the closet."

"Let them wait."

"It's not here anyway." If possible, her fury level went from a ten to an eleven. They could think she'd gotten rid of the laptop and staged this whole mess. "Let's look in the living room and kitchen on our way out."

"We think whoever did this must've stolen the laptop," Cace told Agent Fowler, who waited on the porch. "You're welcome to go and look for it. The bleach is bad in there right now."

"Bynam mentioned what Crime Scene found. I don't have any reason to believe you did this to yourself to make it look like you got burglarized. You would've staged a burglary, not a wholesale destruction of your stuff." What appeared to be sympathy hung in the agent's eyes.

So generous. Sunny shook herself. No need to take out her anger on the guy.

"Let me know if you find your laptop," Fowler continued. "We'll be following up on what we discussed earlier." He paused, then said, "Be careful. You might have someone who doesn't like you very much."

Ya think? "Thanks," she said dryly. Just her landlord's pervy nephew.

Landlord.

Yikes! Surely Ms. Randle would've shown up by now with all the activity. Maybe she had her television up too loud again. "We should let Ms. Randle know what's going on."

Cace walked with her to the front of the house. Television drama music and car crashes practically vibrated the window's glass. Sunny pushed the doorbell with little hope the older woman would hear the chime. Cace knocked hard enough on the thick wood front door that the solid *thunks* made Sunny's knuckles hurt.

Ms. Randle didn't come to the door.

Sunny pulled her phone from her purse and called her landlord's number. No answer. Weird. Sunny left a brief message requesting a callback. Should she use her key? Ms. Randle had given her one to put up the mail when she traveled. The older woman regularly fell asleep in her chair and often failed to charge her mobile phone. If she didn't call back in a couple of hours, Sunny would ask Cace if they should do a welfare check.

He linked his fingers with hers. "My sergeant told me to take the rest of the shift off to handle this business. Let's find what we can salvage and get packed. We can't stay here tonight."

She gritted her teeth. Damn Walter Randle. While she and her boyfriend rounded the corner, she envisioned all the Krav Maga moves she'd use on the pervert. If she ever saw that weasel again, he'd better worry about his ability to father children.

CHAPTER 15

By sheer luck, the rest of Cace's uniforms were due to be picked up at the dry cleaner tomorrow morning, so at least those had been spared, unlike most of the civilian clothing.

Sunny rolled her suitcase into the extended-stay hotel room. The small bag contained what she could salvage from the dresser and bathroom. The medium-sized bag held exercise clothing, makeup, a couple of t-shirts, and pairs of shorts. No scrubs, which she'd need for tomorrow. In her arm, she carried a bag with new toothbrushes for her and Cace, along with shampoo, toothpaste, and other necessities.

Cace allowed the door to swing shut behind him as he wheeled his own suitcase and carried a bag of light groceries they might need until what to do could be determined.

Sunny continued around a built-in eating table, into the bedroom, where she placed her bag in a corner, then deposited the toiletries on the bathroom counter. *Ugh.* The fury began to wear thin, allowing exhaustion to build in her shoulders.

Her phone rang and Sunny dug it out of her purse still slung on her shoulder. "Hello?"

"Sunny? This is Margie Randle. Sorry I missed your message. Looks like you called about two hours ago? What can I help you with?"

Thank goodness. Sunny had been about to ask Cace about the welfare check. "Yes ma'am. I wanted to let you know we have a slight problem at the apartment."

"Oh, dear. I'm not home right now."

Strange. Usually Ms. Randle advised Sunny when she'd be gone. Maybe she had a family emergency. "Is everything okay?"

"I'm at my cousin Ruby's." She exhaled an audible breath. "I didn't want to scare you, but I had to leave my apartment for a bit."

Scare me? "We thought you were home. We heard your television going."

"That's what I want Walter to think. That I'm at home."

"Walter? Is he causing you trouble?" What had that creep done now? "Why didn't you tell me or Cace?"

A pause. "I didn't want to bother you. He's caused you enough trouble. Early this afternoon he came to the apartment and caused a scene. I wouldn't let him in after how ugly he was on Saturday about you. I told him I'd call the police if he didn't leave."

Holy cheezus. Why hadn't Sunny heard that? She must've left the apartment to see Karena by then? "Ms. Randle, I came home about four this afternoon to find my apartment trashed. He smashed my television, and everything from our mattress to our clothing is destroyed."

A longer pause. "He accused me of taking your side over his. That you were lying. I have to think he's the one who broke into your apartment."

"We suspect him too. Also…" She hated to add to the woman's guilt about her nephew.

"I'm sorry dear, are you still there?"

Say it. "The police found cameras in a couple of the air conditioning vents. I think he may have installed them Friday night."

Ms. Randle gasped. "Oh, Sunny. I am so sorry."

The break in the woman's voice nearly fractured Sunny's heart. "It's not your fault, Ms. Randle." Sunny could only imagine how her landlord felt. "You had no way of knowing he'd do this."

"I brought him to your door." Her voice became small.

"You and Cace both said he hadn't done something like that in a long time. You're a sweet lady and tried to give him a break. I don't blame you."

"Regardless, you let me know what needs to be done to fix the apartment, and I'll arrange for the contractors."

"We can talk about that tomorrow. He dumped a lot of bleach and cut up our mattress, so we're at a hotel. I want to sit and not think about this for tonight." Yeah. Like that would happen.

"I understand, dear. Call me tomorrow with what the apartment needs and how long you'll have to stay at the hotel for the damage to be fixed."

After she said goodbye, Sunny punched the red dot on her screen. Unbelievable. Walter needed to be stopped. While she wanted to place his arrest at the top of her agenda, she had to call Sherry next. With Malcolm out, Sunny probably couldn't take the day off. Maybe if the schedule was light, she could leave early. She scrolled through her contacts.

"Hello, Sunny," Sherry said when she answered the phone.

"Hi. I apologize for calling on a Sunday. I have a question about the schedule. Is there a way I might be able to take tomorrow off? I know Malcolm's on leave, so the schedule's probably pretty tight. Someone broke into my apartment, and they trashed everything. I'm going to have to do a lot of cleanup." Each time she thought about the mess or mentioned it to someone, the sheer time and emotional energy she'd have to invest made the task more daunting.

"Oh, wow. Didn't that happen last year?" Sherry's voice sounded sincere, but Sunny couldn't help the niggle that her supervisor doubted her veracity in using such an extreme excuse a second time.

"Yes. My landlady's nephew has turned into a stalker." To add weight to validate her claim, she said, "He smashed our television, ripped our mattress, broke almost every dish. Thank goodness we have renters insurance." Wait. She and Sherry were about the same size. "If I can't have tomorrow off, can I borrow a set of scrubs? He poured bleach on all of my clothing, including my scrubs."

Her supervisor *tsked*. "I wish I could give you a day off. The appointments are tight. You'll at least have to come in the morning. We always have one or two cancellations and I should be able to reschedule some of your afternoon appointments so you can leave early. And I can loan you a set of scrubs until you can buy a couple for yourself."

Sherry seemed to believe her. Relief, as well as a bit of surprise, stole some of the tension in Sunny's shoulders. "Thank you. I really appreciate your help."

"I'm your supervisor. I'm supposed to help. We in the amputee rehab clinic take care of each other."

Amputee. The stolen information. Sunny bit back the words forming on her tongue, those which would alert Sherry to the investigation. Agent Fowler warned her not to discuss the matter with anyone. Shoot. This was her clinic, and she should know of the investigation. No, Sherry could also be a suspect, or they could've already interviewed her. If she already knew and Sunny mentioned the meeting, she'd look bad to her boss. Best to keep mum. Probably screwed either way.

"Sunny?"

Sherry's use of her name pulled Sunny from her whirlwind thoughts. "Sorry. I really appreciate your help. I'll see you tomorrow."

She shoved her phone in the back pocket of her shorts and wandered back into the living area to find Cace sitting on the couch, his eyes glued to his phone. He hadn't bothered to take his suitcase into the bedroom yet.

"What's got you so enthralled?"

His gaze lifted briefly, then dipped back to the screen. "I caught the brand of the camera Perez found."

Sunny dropped into the boxy side chair. "They should make you a detective."

"I have a year before I can take the sergeant's test, then detective after that." A corner of his lips lifted.

He worked hard, and pride filled her heart, because she held no doubt he'd advance. "Still, they're missing out."

He grunted softly and pushed the button to lock his screen, his eyes distant.

After several seconds, Sunny asked, "What'd you find?"

He refocused on her. "It's a cheap brand. I'm pretty sure the model I saw in the bag wouldn't send a signal beyond a hundred feet, especially with interference."

"That's not far. And what would interfere?"

"Walls with significant insulation, piping, electrical wiring, metal, that kind of thing." His lips flattened. "It means the receiver has to be close."

Close. "The house sits on a double lot. Would the signal extend to the street or alley?"

"Maybe the alley, but the distance would be at the end of the range. The cameras were high up, in metal venting and behind the vent covers. The ground rises a bit to the back. So between the metal ducts, the vent covers and the walls, I'd think the alley would be a stretch."

Sunny considered his words. If the signal didn't reach to the street, the receiver had to be really close. "It's in the house?"

"Somewhere close because it has to have power. He may have planted the receiver in our apartment, come back for it, got on a destruction kick, and forgot the cameras."

In the house. "Ms. Randle just called me back. She said Walter came over this afternoon and pitched a fit when she wouldn't let him in. He'd gotten ugly on Friday, so she'd told him to not come back. She threatened to call the police to get him to leave." Oh wow. Energy buzzed through her. "What if…what if the receiver is in her apartment and he tried to get it today? She's got loads of knick-knacks and personal items—maybe he found a place to hide the receiver?"

Cace jumped to his feet. "I'm going to change," he said, and he grabbed his suitcase. He started for the bedroom. "Can you call her and ask if we can check her apartment?"

"Will do." Finally. Something to do other than take Walter's crap beyond mentioning him as a suspect to the police. She pulled her phone from her back pocket and dialed Ms. Randle's number.

And got voicemail.

Cheese and crackers. Sunny left a message, and some of her excitement diminished. What if Ms. Randle didn't see her voicemail? Sunny checked the time. Almost seven o'clock. Her landlady often went to sleep early, sometimes as early as eight. Granted, her going to bed meant falling asleep in front of the television in her easy chair with the volume blaring. Hopefully she'd have her phone close.

Cace reentered the living space in jeans and a t-shirt, striding to the built-in dining table to swipe his truck's keys from the top. When he turned, the slight protrusion at the back of his waistband screamed 'gun.'

He didn't typically carry when off-duty.

The import crashed into her and she shivered. Cace considered Walter dangerous. With luck, they wouldn't need a weapon tonight. Though lately, her luck had been crummy.

"That was quick," Sunny said, then she jumped to her feet. "Ms. Randle didn't answer. I had to leave a message. I hope she calls tonight."

He swore a low oath. "Come on. We need to get your truck anyway for tomorrow. If I heard right, you still have to go to work?"

"Yep." Sunny pulled on the hotel room's door until the heavy panel shut behind her, then tested the handle. "Sherry said she had a set of scrubs I could use, thank goodness."

Cace held the heavy metal-and-glass exit door for her. "Let's check our apartment first. Maybe Perez mistook the receiver for a cable box or something. That way when you talk to Ms. Randle you have more ammunition to justify asking to go into her apartment."

"Maybe we can open some windows while we look. Get some cleanup started while we wait." Beginning to erase Walter from their apartment would feel good. She climbed up into the passenger seat of Cace's truck.

"Good idea." He swung the door shut.

Finally. She moved forward. The energy of purpose buoyed her past the crushing feeling of victimhood and rage.

Cace climbed in the truck. "Are you humming?"

She smiled at him. "It's a victory tune."

"Don't count your chickens before they've hatched. We could be wrong."

Certainty coalesced in her stomach. She'd never felt so right.

CHAPTER 16

Sunny shut the door to the washer and pressed the 'on' button, then shut the bi-fold doors which concealed her laundry area. Over the last two hours, they'd searched the apartment for the receiver without luck. Cace checked the other vents, pulled at carpeting for secret trap doors, examined the underside of furniture, even scouted out the inside of the fireplace behind the coal insert.

No receiver.

And fortunately, no more cameras. After that, he went outside with a flashlight to see if maybe Walter had attached the electronic device to the house in an unobtrusive way. Maybe he'd found one with batteries or somehow constructed a power supply.

Luckily, she'd found more salvageable clothing. While she'd packed a good portion of the ruined garments into large black trash bags to be discarded, what she'd been able to save went into the washer. Mercifully, one set of scrubs survived with only a couple of small bleach spots on the hem, not really noticeable. Two pairs of jeans made the cut, too, one hers, one Cace's. No underwear though. It all got thrown away. She didn't want to have to wear bras or panties which reminded her Walter had seen or touched them.

She pushed back the fury at the idea. No. She had purpose now. And that, rather than rage, would drive her. Yet, the anger was hard to maintain when Ms. Randle still hadn't called back. By Sunny's phone, the time read five after nine o'clock.

The front door opened, and her heart slammed against her chest.

"Sunny?" Cace called.

Thank goodness. "Here," she said, making her way along the path she'd cleared through the chaos on the kitchen floor and rounding the corner into the dining area. "Did you find anything?"

He shook his head negatively. "Did Ms. Randle call back?"

"Not yet." Concern and frustration ate at her will to remain positive. "I had an idea that if he still needs to get the receiver, maybe he didn't see us changing or doing…"

He looked at her with narrowed eyes, almost as if he didn't recognize her. "How can you stay so positive? After all that's gone on?"

A little laugh escaped her. She didn't like the despair the strangled sound held. "If I'm not positive, I'd probably have lost my mind by now," she said with an attempt at a casual shrug. "After what's gone on in the last year, first with Ben and Abby, then the murders down in Carson, I'd go nuts. Maybe I am. I claim to have some psychic power to find things."

He righted a dining room chair, then pulled her to sit on his lap, his strong arms circling her with their promise of security.

She rested her cheek against the soft material of his t-shirt while the tension started to drain away.

"You're not losing your mind or a nut." He kissed the top of her head. "I'm not going to lie. Sometimes I've been mad at your Gift. It's put you in dangerous spots. But I love you, Gift and all. At least you're not seeing ghosts, right?"

Like Mina.

"Or having to process visions of people dying."

Like Lacey did sometimes.

She sighed, the rest of her frustration released with the breath. She shifted a little so she could see his face. "Thank you. I love you too. You're the best partner a woman could have."

He dipped his head for a kiss which held sweetness and love.

Once the kiss ended, she hugged him closer and placed her cheek against his shoulder. "I'm done with the apartment tonight. I don't think Ms. Randle's going to call. She usually goes to sleep pretty early and with all the excitement, she may have been overwhelmed and went to bed earlier than normal."

"Probably. I'll follow you to the hotel, then come back and make sure Walter doesn't try to break into her apartment."

She sat up straighter. No way she'd spend tonight alone. Or allow Cace to do the same. When she went back to the hotel, she'd planned to ask him to make sure there weren't cameras in the room. A silly idea, but the creep factor would linger.

"I'm staying with you."

"I don't know if it's a good idea."

His immovable-object stance pricked her unstoppable-force nature. "Why not?"

"He may show up. If I were him, I'd try to jimmy her back door or break a window, probably in her kitchen, furthest from the living room and the television. Assuming he's aware she largely sleeps in her easy chair."

"And if he doesn't know that?"

"I'd probably go for a side window. Glass breaking is always tricky. Done right, the sound is minimal. If he hears the television, he may assume she's still in the living room, so I'm betting on the back of the house."

Logical. "Okay. Where are we going to sit?"

He let out a heavy breath. "You're not going to change your mind, are you?"

"No. Honestly? I'm too creeped out to sleep alone. So if you're here, I'm here."

"I guess I can understand that. I don't know that sleep was in the cards for me tonight either." He framed her shoulders with his hands and leveled her a solemn gaze. "You have to promise you'll let me do the work. All you'll do is call the police. Promise?"

She nodded as some Krav Maga moves snuck their way into her thoughts.

He lifted a brow. "Promise?"

"Yes, dang it. I promise."

"Good. Let's take our trucks and park them on Fuller Street." He hooked a thumb over his shoulder to the houses which backed up to the alley. "That way he'll assume we're gone and may be more likely to break in."

"Even with Jason and Will at home? Duh," she said immediately. "Not like that stopped him before." The cars for the renters in the two upper units were still in the small parking area.

"I saw Jason rolling a big suitcase before I left for work on Wednesday. He got in the back of a car. I bet he's away. And Will got another government contract, so he's been gone for three weeks already, probably six more like his usual tours."

Wow. She rarely saw either man and had hardly noticed when they left. And Will lived directly above her. She needed to up her observation skills. "Okay. Let's move the cars. What then?"

"Then we wait."

Five minutes later, she pulled her truck behind Cace's onto Fuller Street, one block north of the Victorian.

Cace joined her on the pavement as she shut her door. "Here." He handed her a spray can and a black ball cap.

She donned the hat, pulling her blonde ponytail halfway through the hole to keep the long strands restrained, then studied the thin cylinder in what illumination could be garnered from the distant street light. "Mosquito repellent?"

"We're waiting in the gazebo. You'll get eaten alive."

True enough. Sprayed down with the unscented mist, she handed the can back to Cace, who sprayed himself, then put the cylinder back in his truck's console and shut the door. The long way around the block and through the alley put them closest to the corner of the yard with the gazebo, the corner furthest from the side street.

Cace carefully pushed apart some bushes at the back of the property meant for privacy. The gazebo lay directly ahead, through the short, scratchy avenue.

"Why can't we go around?" she whispered.

"He may already be casing the house. Probably not, because he's lazy. Best not to take a chance. He'll look for signs of life in our apartment and assume since our vehicles are gone, we are too."

Great. She wished she'd chosen jeans and a long-sleeved shirt. But she'd asked to be here. She edged through, sucking in a breath when a twig poked into her shin, probably drawing blood. Otherwise, she made her way through the barrier largely unscathed, then waited for

Cace to join her. No one would see them and call the police, right?

Once through the hedge, he skirted the edge of the plantings, then crossed the ten yards to the gazebo. She followed his sprint and stooped low. He vaulted over the railing and landed in a crouch on the little structure's floorboards.

Impressive. And not something she'd be able to do. Feeling quite silly, she scrambled over as best she could, trying to keep down. She joined him on the back bench. From this angle, she could see both the side and rear to Ms. Randle's apartment. The light at her landlord's back door didn't reach all the twenty or so yards to the gazebo. Even so, Sunny thanked her luck for wearing a dark gray shirt with A-R-M-Y in black. She should blend in. A bare glimmer at the bottom of her vision made her grimace. Reflective tape on her running shoes. Great. Hopefully Walter didn't have eagle eyes.

She shifted her focus to Cace, who practically blended into the shadows in his dark jeans and black t-shirt. Of course. She leaned and murmured into his ear. "You knew you were staying tonight, didn't you?"

"Shh," he whispered back.

Tricky man. She sat back against the railing to wait. Sunny bet Walter would come from the alley. Even though Ms. Randle closed her blinds, light still escaped. If Walter tried to access those windows, maybe someone from the street would see. On the Victorian's rear face, the kitchen windows sat dark, the only illumination coming from what had to be the sixty-watt bulb in the porch light next to her screen door. Across the entirety of the yard, enough plantings and trees ensured headlights from cars turning onto the side street wouldn't reveal Sunny and Cace. Or Walter, for that matter, if he chose to approach from the alley.

Sunny searched the shadows for a hint of movement, growing tense during the wait.

The breeze from the evening died. Cars drove by in front of the house. Small animals snuffled through the underbrush. A mosquito who desperately wanted to land on her droned in her ear.

A dog barked in the house behind her, and her heart jumped, thump-thumping hard in her chest. *Cheese and crackers.*

"Try not to move." Cace whispered.

Right. That dog scared her half to death. How long had she been waiting? Not like she could check the time. Her phone's screen would give her away.

Cace placed a hand on her bouncing knee, then leaned over slowly, his lips finally ending at her ear. "It's ten o'clock. We may be here for a while."

Mortification shot through her. She hadn't realized she'd been moving like that. And how did he know she wanted to know the time? Maybe he remembered when he started these types of surveillances in the Army. Waiting sucked. Rather than responding, she covered his hand with hers and squeezed her acknowledgement.

While she resumed searching the shadows for a hint of movement, she mentally ran through some self-defense moves. If she needed them, she better be able to act this time. *No more Miss Nice-Lady, remember?* Cace and her instructor said to go over the actions in her mind too. That visualization would help train her brain in what to do. Though the practice hadn't worked a couple of days ago, a new determination filled her. Even if all she was supposed to do was call 9-1-1 while Cace faced the real danger, she wouldn't freeze again.

What could've been half an hour or four hours later, Cace tensed next to her.

What had he heard? She wanted to sit up straighter, yet didn't dare move now. The faint crackle of dry vegetation cut into the still night.

The hairs on her arms stood at attention. A tall, bulky shadow moved at the edge of the parking area. Too big for an animal. Human.

Her heart started to thunder in her ears. She lost sight of the figure when the shadow blended into the tall bushes at the back of the property. Would the person go away? For several seconds she strained her eyes, searching for any hint of where the shadow might appear. Not fifteen yards from the gazebo, a thick, straight stick raised from the gloom, pointing toward the back of the house.

A stick? That didn't make sense.

Of course, it didn't. It only made perfect sense if the stick was a gun.

CHAPTER 17

Pfft. Pfft. Pfft. Tink.

The light on Ms. Randle's back porch winked out after the third shot.

Sunny's mouth dried. Holy cheezus. He'd shot out the porch light.

Thank the sweet Lord Cace brought his gun. She eased back from where she'd unintentionally leaned forward. From her periphery, Cace hadn't seemed to move, let alone drawn his gun. She reviewed the earlier sounds. Much more like a pellet gun rather than the loud report of a rifle. Cace must've come to the same conclusion.

The knowledge didn't lessen her tension. The person had yet to make a move, possibly waiting to see if anyone noticed and came to investigate. Minutes ticked by, which seemed more like hours.

Finally, the bulky form detached itself from the bushes' deep shadows and moved swiftly to the back door. The slightest creak of the screen door's hinges shot through the night. Hesitation. Then the shape jostled a little bit. Maybe trying to force the door open?

Cace gained his feet in a flash. His silent steps crossed the distance with surprising speed.

With trembling fingers, Sunny pulled her phone from her back pocket. She'd wait until he announced himself.

Her boyfriend's taller, thinner outline crossed the scant light emitted by the side windows on his way toward the person at the door. "Police. Put your hands up," Cace said, at the same time he used a flashlight's blinding beam to illuminate the figure.

Walter. He put his hands up, a foot-long bar in his hand instead of an air rifle—where had the gun gone?

"Stay where you are, Walter Randle."

Sunny dialed 9-1-1 like she'd promised.

"Walter. Stop," Cace's voice bellowed.

Sunny shot to her feet. Cace's beam bounced while he raced after the other man, who ran in the direction of the parking lot.

Oh, no. Walter was getting away. She started sprinting after Cace.

"Nine-one-one. What's your emergency?"

Sunny swallowed to wet her suddenly dry mouth. "We just caught someone breaking into our neighbor's apartment. My boyfriend's Cace Navarro. He works for Belton Police. He's running after the man—Walter Randle."

"What's your address?" The operator's tone changed from professionally bored to urgent.

Sunny provided the address, then pounded after the pair. "Walter is running, ah, north, toward Spring—wait, he's turned, ah, west on Spring."

"Stay on the line, and let me know any other details." Then the dispatcher's voice sounded distant, calling for all available units to respond.

Beginning to lag behind, Sunny upped her pace. Good gravy. Walter sure could run fast for an overweight man.

Though if he wanted to avoid arrest, he had good motivation.

A street light showed Walter turned right. "He's in the alley north of..." What street had she parked her truck on? "North of Fuller Street."

"Thank you." The woman's voice murmured in the background.

As she rounded the corner, Sunny started sucking for serious air—along with her sprinting, the excitement must've pushed adrenaline into her system. She stopped about two houses down the dim alley. Where had Cace's flashlight gone?

"Ma'am?"

"Yes?" Sunny said.

"Do you have an update?"

"No, I've lost them. I don't see Cace's light at all." She searched frantically through the shadows. Maybe Walter jumped a fence and cut through a yard?

"Okay. Please let me know."

Goosebumps broke out over her body while she continued to look for Cace. She shouldn't be here. In an alley with no light. Almost all of the yards had high fences.

With a creep like Walter on the loose.

Her stomach cramped with the realization, and she took a couple of steps back.

A crunch of gravel alerted her to someone who approached from behind, but not fast enough. A hard clamp bore down on her arm while a hand slapped over her mouth. "Drop the phone," Walter snarled in her ear.

She froze. No. How…

Something sharp poked her in the side. "I said drop the fucking phone, bitch."

The violence in his voice broke her from her frozen state and prompted her to move. She tossed the phone toward the side of the alley, hoping it would land somewhere soft and the dispatcher would still hear her.

"Give me the thumb drive."

The thumb drive? Why would he want a thumb drive with patient information? "What?"

"Give me the thumb drive. I know you have it."

"I don't—"

The point dug into her side. "Don't lie to me. I saw you with it. You parked next to me at the restaurant. You don't have a Fiber-Now account, and those are the free ones we give away."

She'd already given the device to the agents. What about the other one? The one she gave to Ms. Randle? *Buy time. Get back somewhere safer than this alley. Maybe Cace will find me.* "At the apartment. In my purse."

"Good. Now don't make a sound, and I won't have to stab you."

The sharp point disappeared from her side, as did the hand from her mouth.

Move now!

She twisted away from the side he held the blade, hitting at the side of his neck with her forearm. She stopped her spin, feet soundly under her, hands up in a defensive position. "Help! Walter Randle has a knife!" she yelled while taking steps backward. She had to keep on her feet. Hopefully, someone could hear her cries.

He still had the blade and stood there for a moment, possibly uncertain of what to do now. Maybe her blow to his neck connected a bit.

"Help! Help! He has a weapon!" Get to safety. She couldn't turn her back. Instead, she kept retreating toward the entrance to the alley, careful step after careful step.

He shook his head like a bull ready to charge the cape,

then he rushed forward. The quarter moon's shadows added to the savagery in his face.

Closer. Defend. Attack. She waited. She waited even when Walter brought the knife down from overhead. Time slowed. Still she waited. At the last moment, she whirled away to the side of his empty hand. Pushed him in the back and he continued forward.

Facing him, she got her feet under her shoulders again, and brought her hands up.

But he'd fallen to the ground. The shove worked. *Run now!* She raced to her phone where the light still glowed from the grass, scooped up her mobile, and sprinted toward the alley's other end.

"He's in the same alley near Spring," she said into her phone. Almost to the street and possible safety.

A dark figure loomed in front of her, and she skidded to a stop several feet away. She dropped her phone and assumed the ready stance.

Walter wouldn't get her this time either.

CHAPTER 18

Wait. This figure didn't have a chubby middle. His hands were held above his shoulders.

Sunny's name came to her ears as if shouted from a mile away, then became louder.

Flashing red-and-blue lights from behind her lit the figure's face.

Cace.

She launched herself at him. Strong arms wrapped around her, and she buried her face in his neck.

While he spoke to her, his words came in garbled, but she wasn't letting go. Not right now. Finally, she made out that he asked, "Are you okay?"

Though she didn't want to release him, she pulled back and gazed up. "I'm fine."

He looked ready to say something when a male voice shouted from the other end of the alley. "Navarro."

"We've got to go." He put her gently on her feet.

Her knees wobbled, and she struggled to stay upright since her whole body decided to start shivering. "O-Okay," she said through chattering teeth. What the heck?

He snugged her to his side while he moved forward

slowly, supporting her. "You're on the downside of an adrenaline dump. Very common after the fight-or-flight mechanism kicks you in the gut."

She clung to his waist. Together, they made their way to the end of the alley where Walter lay on his stomach, his wrists handcuffed at his back. The knife lay on the hood of the patrol car, encased in a plastic bag. Sunny sucked a breath at the weapon's size. The blade seemed big enough to gut an elephant. If she'd known it was *that* big, she might've lost her nerve.

Walter glanced up at her, a sneer on his face displayed by the police car's headlights. A wound on his forehead bled overtop a significant bump. He must've hit his head when he went down. Satisfaction crawled through her. Good. While she may not have eliminated his chances at siring children, at least she'd put the hurt on him. She didn't break eye contact with the pervert and sneered back, breaking only when Officer Bynam asked, "What happened?"

Cace started the narrative with his discovery of the cameras' ranges and his thinking about where the receiver could be. Sunny added her conversation with Ms. Randle, careful not to let Walter know exactly where the woman had fled. Cace picked the story up again, leading all the way to when he lost Walter after running through the alley.

"I followed, then realized I shouldn't be in a dark alley all alone," Sunny said, following with the details of Walter's attack. Cace stiffened next to her.

She glanced up, but he didn't direct his anger at her. Cace stared at the stalker handcuffed on the ground like he wanted to give him a good kick.

Bynam said, "You did really well. Not many people would've thought so fast."

Her teeth still wanted to chatter, so she answered his praise with a mere nod.

Cace hugged her tighter. Silent praise or a need to keep her close? Maybe both. Didn't matter though. Any tighter and she'd pass out from lack of air.

"What's the deal with the thumb drive?" Bynam asked.

"I found one in the Tipsy Burro's parking lot. He was there eating with his aunt. I saw him, but he's such a creep, I didn't want to talk to him." She spat the words out and looked down at the man. "I have no idea why he wanted it back so badly. I gave the drive to his aunt yesterday. As far as I know, it's still in her house."

Walter groaned.

Another police SUV with lights flashing rolled up at the end of the alley. 'Supervisor' had been stenciled on the front bumper. A uniformed woman stepped out.

"Sergeant," Cace used a pronunciation closer to what Sunny typically heard in the VA from the soldiers, sounding more like 'sar-dent' with a soft, slurred 'd'. This must be Sergeant Adams, Cace's shift supervisor. Surely, she wouldn't be mad he'd lain in wait for Walter?

Sergeant Adams nodded at Cace's address, then also took in Sunny's form. "Everyone okay?"

"We are," Cace said, looking down at her.

Sunny nodded, ponytail bouncing against her neck. "Yep. Just a little scare."

"I'm going to have him taken to the ER to get his head checked out," Bynam said with no small amount of disgust. "Then I'll take him down and book him for assault."

"Not burglary?" Sunny asked, surprised.

"When we can get ahold of Mrs. Randle," Cace said. "She'll have to be the complainant, since he tried to break into her apartment. You told Bynum he assaulted you with a deadly weapon."

"You want to make a statement tonight, Sunny?" The sergeant's mouth slanted a smile. "My apologies." She held out her right hand. "Wanda Adams. You must be Cace's Sunny."

"Sunny Flannigan, ma'am." She accepted the other woman's hand.

"Would you like to come down to make a statement tonight or tomorrow?"

Exhaustion tugged at Sunny's shoulders. She wouldn't last ten minutes without face-planting into the table. "I'd like to come tomorrow afternoon, if I could. I'm exhausted."

Sergeant Adams nodded, then turned to Officer Bynam. "Let's get him on his feet and to the ER, then book him, aggravated assault, deadly weapon."

Sunny turned to Cace. "I think I'm ready to go back to the hotel. Or is there still something we have to do?"

"Not until Ms. Randle calls you back." Cace hugged her a little closer, a wan smile on his lips. "I think we need to get you to bed. You still have work tomorrow."

Not that she'd ever get to sleep again, what with a foot chase, Walter's attack, and her victory over the freezes. On the walk to the trucks, she pulled her phone from her pocket to check the time. Two-thirty. Oh, boy. Out of nowhere, her lids drooped, she stifled a huge yawn, and she felt as if she slogged through waist-deep water to merely walk.

"You want me to drive us back? I can drop you at your truck tomorrow morning."

"But you won't get to sleep in."

"I don't need much sleep. You know that."

True enough. She assented. Once inside the vehicle, she buckled the seatbelt with leaden arms.

For several minutes, Cace drove in silence. "Can I say one thing, then I'll leave it alone?"

She rolled her head against the headrest to the left. *That* didn't sound ominous at all. "I guess."

"I really wish you would've stayed put and called the police like I requested. Walter could've killed you."

Like I didn't know that was coming. He had a point, though. Walter could've killed her. "In my defense, you didn't mention staying put. You said call the police and let you handle Walter. The operator asked where you went, so I followed." He opened his mouth to say something, but she plowed on. "If it makes you feel any better, I learned my lesson." She rolled her head back and closed her eyes. "Going down that alley was stupid. I recognized my mistake and had turned to leave. Somehow he got behind me."

He paused for a moment. More lecture? A long exhale. "You are going to be the death of me. How can I protect you if you don't stay put?"

"You did protect me. Without you, I wouldn't have had the Krav Maga classes and wouldn't have been able to defend myself. I froze at first, then reflex kicked in. Move away from the knife or gun. Defend, then attack. To bring him down was worth every miserable, muscle cramping, big-bruises minute. How did you lose him anyway? You're fast. I thought you would've caught him with no problem."

"Nice job at changing the subject." Cace shook his head with a huffed laugh. "He got a lead when I holstered my gun. Not smart to run with your weapon drawn if you can help it. You heard the rest. He rounded a corner, I lost him, and followed where I thought he would've gone."

He covered her hand with his. "If I ever get to meet this Gift of yours, I'll…" he murmured.

"You'll what?" Sunny laughed.

"I'm going to punch it in the face for all the worry it's cause me and the scares it's given you."

Sunny smiled and closed her eyes. The idea sure had merit.

CHAPTER 19

Sunny smothered a yawn with the back of her hand, pushed down the lock button, and shut her truck's door. Three and a half hours. That's how much sleep she managed to get last night.

She and Cace went out at sunrise to show a detective what they'd seen. The officers found an air rifle deep in some overgrown rose bushes not far from where Walter had stood to shoot out the light. Pry marks on Ms. Randle's back door most likely came from the crowbar laying on the grass halfway to the parking lot. The tool possibly might match the damage on Sunny's door too. She'd gotten the scrubs from the dryer, the set serviceable, if a little wrinkled. Hopefully, Sherry wouldn't be upset she brought a pair in for no good reason.

A deep breath and a sip from her pumpkin spice latte gave Sunny a little energy bump. She trooped across the parking lot and badged her way into the building. At her locker, she set her coffee and purse on the bench, which ran between the rows, then turned her lock tumblers to her combination. She picked up her purse to place it inside. The bottom of her bag caught the large cup of coffee and the plastic lid separated from the paper cup. Coffee splashed everywhere, including across the legs of the one set of scrubs she'd been able to salvage.

She stared at the green and white cup, then the spreading mess of milk, sugar, and caffeine. Any remaining energy drained from her. Of course she would spill her coffee today when she needed the caffeine the most. No employee willingly drank the snack bar's coffee. She'd swear they filtered the brew with a teen's used athletic sock. The coffee vending machine didn't provide a much better cup. Cheese and crackers. Vending machine it would have to be. She set her purse on her locker's shelf to get the bag out of the way.

She rounded the corner to the sinks. With some water, she blotted at the dark splotches in the light blue scrubs, then pushed the lever until she had a wad of the cheap brown paper towels in her hands. Typical government purchase. She'd need at least double what she used at home. She dabbed at her scrubs, then took more to clean up the bigger mess. Maybe she'd need Sherry's pair after all.

With a giant pile of the crappy towels in hand, she rounded the corner to the squeal of the main door's hinge. She crossed the end of the two rows of lockers. Huh. No one. Someone didn't come in, they left. Probably saw the coffee, thought 'not my circus,' and did an about-face.

She mopped up the mess as best as possible. Next stop would be a call to housekeeping. They were pretty strict about who did what, or Sunny would find a janitor's closet, grab some cleaning spray, and clean up the sticky mess herself. She shut her locker and started to set the lock. Wait a minute. She opened the door again.

Her purse. Where was her purse?

What the…? The locker room door. The mysterious

someone hadn't seen the coffee and left. They'd stolen her purse from her locker's ledge.

She lifted her eyes to the ceiling and took a deep, calming breath. Though incredibly tired, she'd still had a win over Walter last night and had been feeling pretty good about herself. This knocked the wind right out of her windmill blades. And for someone she worked with to be the thief too. Granted, locks on the lockers had been recommended for a reason. Didn't they know the place was riddled with security cameras? Maybe this person knew some of them worked, others didn't, as Sunny recently learned. Not like she had much money, though her checkbook and debit card necessitated a call to the bank.

A stray wisp of hair tickled her ear, and she tucked the strand back with a sigh. Better go tell Sherry.

"Knock, knock," Sunny said at her supervisor's door.

Sherry swiveled in her chair and took in Sunny's form. "I brought a pair of scrubs. Did you find some you could use?"

"Yeah, but I spilled coffee all over them in the locker room." Sunny pursed her lips and gestured to the damp, dark brown-blue splotches on her pants. "While I cleaned up at the sink, someone came in and stole my purse."

"Oh for…" Sherry's voice trailed off with a murmured curse, and she picked up the handset to her phone. "You have the worst luck."

"Yeah, lately it seems that way."

Her supervisor punched a couple of buttons. "Hey, it's Sherry. We've got a problem. Someone stole one of my therapist's purses from the women's locker room."

A nudge hit Sunny hard in the left shoulder. She turned to see who'd punched her. No one. Her fingers started burning.

Not now. She'd finally gotten to what might be a good

place with Sherry and someone stole her purse. A doubly-bad time.

The next 'nudge' almost knocked her off-balance, and the heat in her fingers blossomed into flame. *Ow.* Sunny flexed her hands. This had never happened before. Could the Gift be sending her toward her purse? The nudge hit her again, this time not as hard.

Sherry hung up the phone. "Security said the cameras in front of the locker rooms have been down for a while. He wants you to come down to make a report."

If related to her purse, Sunny had to follow the Gift's directions. She may run the risk of ruining a tenuous relationship with her supervisor, though Sunny had little choice because she may need a witness. "Sherry, could you come with me?"

Her supervisor cocked her head at the request. "Sure." The way she drew out the word indicated she believed the request strange.

"Good. We have to go now." Sunny turned and stared racing in the direction the Gift had told her to go.

"Hey. Wait," Sherry called from behind.

Sunny didn't wait—urgency gripped her. Pressure on her right shoulder caused her to turn at an intersection, toward the old lab, which they were renovating into additional physical therapy space. *Hurry, hurry, hurry*, chanted in her head in time with her tennis shoes pounding on the white-and-gray, linoleum tile. The old lab loomed ahead, a wall of plastic separating the space from the hallway.

"Hey, the security office is the other way," Sherry called from behind her.

Sunny had no time to explain. She burst through a seam in the plastic dust barrier and came to a stop in the middle of the new physical therapy wing. Which way? She scanned the large, open area dotted on the left with doorways into what should be exam rooms. The grid for a drop ceiling had been installed with overhead fluorescents providing lighting. No workers, merely a ladder, boxes of ceiling tiles, and a lot of construction debris.

And one exam room with the lights on.

Cary stopped in the doorway. His eyes narrowed.

She locked gazes with him. Calculation flashed in his eyes, before he smiled, a big, fat, fake grin which no one would believe. "This will be a great place once it's done, right? So much more space to work."

Is my bag in the room Cary just came from? The fire increased in her hands, indicating she was close. A couple of pulses may be the Gift's way of giving a positive answer to her question. "Why did you steal my purse?"

"I didn't steal it." He took several steps forward, then stopped. Her nine-year-old nephew could fake shock better.

"Yes, you did." Certainty solidified in her stomach. "It's behind you in that room."

His jaw locked, and his eyes narrowed. "I don't know what you're talking about."

"Is her purse in the room, Cary?" Sherry said from behind Sunny.

"No." He took several steps from the exam room. "She's obviously lost her mind."

Memories burst into Sunny's vision. Cary pulling up to the parking area on Friday, looking at the ground, asking if she found something. In his shiny new car. Cary at the restaurant at the table next to them, reaching down to pick up a fork he'd dropped…toward her purse. Why would he want her purse? Her fingers pulsed.

The second drive. The one she found in the parking lot.

Confident of her accusation, Sunny said, "You're the one. The one who stole the patient information."

Sherry had crossed to the space between Sunny and Cary. Her brows rose. "How did you know about that?"

"I told you, she's crazy." His tone rose. "I wouldn't steal information."

"Sure you would. Like you stole my purse." Sunny strode toward the room. It had to be in there. She'd appear a fool otherwise. But her Gift told her she'd been right in her accusation and guided her here.

When she passed Cary, he grabbed her arm, though not hard enough she'd need to attack back. Yet. "Let go of me," she said, her tone as hard as her anger.

He dropped his hand like he'd been stung. "Fine." He turned to her supervisor and spread his arms in an appealing gesture at odds with the panic flaring in his eyes. "She's lying."

That's the best he could come up with? "Sherry, could you come in here with me?"

For a second the other woman hesitated, then said, "Sure."

Sunny entered, while Sherry stopped at the doorway.

Inside sat a ladder and a tall, barrel full of construction debris. Pink, fluffy insulation lay atop. Sunny turned the container over and the contents spilled out. Insulation and drywall. No purse. Her stomach curdled, and her gaze leapt to Sherry.

The cautious belief of a minute ago had shifted to a narrow-eyed assessment.

"See," Cary said from the doorway, practically over Sherry's shoulder. "I told you she was lying."

It must be here. Sunny searched the room again, turning over the pile of trash. Frustration built. Other than the barrel and the ladder—

The ladder. She raised her eyes to the newly installed ceiling tiles. Two steps forward and she'd put her foot on the first rung.

"I mean, she's obviously nuts." Cary's voice rose. "I'm leaving."

"Stay, Cary. If that's true, there's nothing to be seen, and I have a witness. If there's a purse up there, we have a problem." Even if her supervisor's statement wasn't an affirmative show of support, Sherry didn't discount Sunny either. Plus, Sherry expressed zero surprise about the data theft, meaning she knew.

Gratified Sherry would at least let her try, Sunny stepped up several rungs until she reached a level where she could move one of the large, rectangular tiles, then continued two more rungs until she could look inside the space.

And there sat her purse.

She looked down at Sherry and nodded.

The other woman's mouth firmed, and she turned to Cary.

He'd already begun to back out of the room, shaking his head, eyes wide. "She planted that," he said, his voice shaking.

"No. I didn't." Sunny dusted her hands off, descended the ladder, and joined Sherry. "And you wouldn't have found the drive in there anyway. I already gave it to the OIG Agents."

"You bitch," Cary bellowed. He charged toward her, his fists raised.

Sunny turned to the side as he reached her, sticking her foot out to trip him.

He fell face first into the new drywall, then slumped on the floor.

Shock coursed through her. Where had that move come from?

During the attack, the less time you have to think, the more likely you are to be successful, because you will come from a place of reaction, rather than trying to figure out which tactic to use. Her Krav Maga instructor's words. And they'd been exactly right. Pure reflex.

Phone to her ear, Sherry took Sunny's arm and backed her up to the plastic barrier. "We'll need security and a medical team. I think when he ran into the wall he hit his head on one of the metal studs."

Cary groaned.

Sunny braced, ready to defend herself again, and Sherry, too, if necessary.

Agent Fowler stepped through the plastic barrier, followed by Agent Brown. Their gazes swept the area. Both started forward. "Cary Larson, you're under arrest."

CHAPTER 20

Sunny fiddled with the vending machine's empty coffee cup, the only object which could occupy her busy hands. Despite the awful taste, she'd take another, except the agents asked she stay put. She'd been in the conference room for an hour.

The door behind her opened, and Sunny spun in her chair toward the sound.

Cace.

She leapt to her feet and fell into his arms.

"What am I going to do with you?" he asked while stroking her back gently.

The comfort reassured her enough to try for humor. "Love me?"

He husked a laugh. "I'll always love you. I just need to set up some sort of protection detail for you."

"You know that's not necessary."

"Isn't it?"

"No. I defended myself fine this time." Pride straightened her spine a bit. She disengaged and led him to where she'd been sitting.

"So Sherry told me," he said with a tight smile while he sank into the padded conference chair next to her.

"Sherry?"

"I tried calling your phone. When you didn't answer, I called Sherry. She told me what happened."

"You know I don't carry my phone with me on the floor." She wanted to give her patients her whole attention.

"I thought I'd try. I have some news." He grinned wide, all teeth like a shark about to sink its jaws into a meaty fish.

She cocked her head and lifted a brow, urging him to continue.

"Right after you left, the detective got a hold of Ms. Randle. She said we could enter, and since the door would probably have to be replaced anyway with the amount of damage, we forced our way in. She told us where she put the hard-drive. And we found the receiver on a table behind some picture frames. He'd made a cable box shell. Even had a sticker that said it was the property of Fiber-Now. We took the receiver back to the office and pulled a similar red-and-silver thumb drive from it." He crossed his arms. "Now I know why he wanted that drive back so bad."

His flat, hard words rattled her. "Why?"

"We aren't the only apartment he put cameras in. There were a bunch of videos on the drive you gave Ms. Randle. The belief right now is he used his cable job to install cameras in other women's apartments. Probably went back a couple days later with an excuse he needed to install better equipment or used some other manufactured reason to pick up the receiver.

Sunny completely believed Walter could conceive of such a plan. Yet, the idea still shocked her. Other women were victims too?

"We won't know until we can ID some of the women

on the video," Cace continued. "Maybe twenty in all. Looks like he took mementos from each residence. Off the drive from the receiver we got from Ms. Randle, I watched him steal our photo after he'd done the camera installation, so he probably did the same thing to other women too. He may have worn gloves during the break-in, but his face is going to be a hard one to deny." A grim half-smile spoke of his satisfaction.

Anger knotted in her gut. The jerk probably enjoyed his job. "It's no wonder so many women don't report creepy servicemen. They're afraid of retaliation, like what he did to our apartment."

"Ah. That's where this gets interesting."

More interesting?

"He broke into our apartment with a small crowbar, like the one we found after he tried to break into Ms. Randle's. He started to climb up to the vents when something scared him. He stopped. A couple of minutes later, he left, without removing the cameras."

What? "I thought he trashed the apartment."

"Not him. Someone else."

"Stop teasing."

"Cary."

She wanted to be shocked, except after he stole her purse this morning, Cary made total sense.

A knock at the door sounded, then Agent Fowler popped his head into the conference room. "Making sure I wasn't interrupting anything." He stepped through, followed by Agent Brown, who carried Sunny's purse in her hand. The two took a seat across from Sunny and Cace.

"Looks like you're off the hook for the medical information theft," Agent Fowler said.

The offhand manner of his announcement grated.

Sunny sat back in her chair and crossed her arms. "I never was on the hook in the first place."

He ignored her comment. "I'm going to need an accounting of what happened today."

"Wait. Cace. Tell them what you told me about Cary."

Cace said, "The video not only caught Sunny's stalker installing the cameras, but also that something startled Walter. He left, then Cary Larson pushed the door open, looked like he called out to see if anyone was there, then stepped inside real quick. By trashing the place, he may have thought to make the simple laptop theft look like a burglary." Cace's lips flattened. "While in the bedroom, he clearly slipped Sunny's laptop under his shirt before he left the apartment."

"Presumably, he thought Sunny accessed or saved the information on her computer," Agent Brown said with an arched eyebrow.

Cace nodded. "My thoughts as well."

"We photographed your purse and can give it back to you." The other woman slid the bag across the table. "However, we would like to know if anything's missing."

Sunny pulled everything out and performed a mental accounting. "Nothing's missing. Checkbook, credit cards, and the four bucks left over from my coffee this morning are still there. The keys are clipped on the lanyard."

"Cary lawyered up, so we're going to need the full story of what happened today."

Sunny complied, minus mentioning the Gift. Odds were, like before, they wouldn't believe her.

Agent Fowler folded his hands together on the conference table's dark wood top and examined her for a moment. "So this *feeling* you said you had on how you found your purse."

"So?"

"Someone stole your purse. Several minutes later you said you had a feeling on where it might be. You ran right to the location. At least that's what Sherry said."

Dang. Sunny would have to credit the Gift again. "What I told you about yesterday, the Gift I have, led me to where Cary hid my purse."

"The gift you have." This time he used air quotes around the words with eyebrows which had climbed over his wire frames.

Practicality snuffed out her annoyance. Of course they continued not to believe in her Gift.

"I don't think she's lying," Cace said. He spread his hands. "Have you ever had that sixth sense something wasn't right? I know I did a lot while deployed. I'd see a situation and something—nothing I could put a finger on directly—said trouble. Nine times out of ten, the little warning sense proved right. I learned to listen and it saved my life a couple of times. Many police officers also believe in a sixth sense. Sometimes we can't explain everything."

Fowler's lips twisted. "You believe her?"

"Absolutely."

"The U.S. Attorney is going to want more than that."

Sunny sat back and crossed her arms. "I can't give them more than the truth."

Agent Brown placed a hand on her coworker's arm. "There are some things you can't explain. From the surveillance system, we observed you walk in with your purse, go down the hallways toward the locker room. We didn't see you again until after Cary walked into the area under construction, a lump under his arm, followed a couple of minutes later by you and Sherry. How you knew to go there, a hunch or logic, is not really relevant."

At least one agent stood in her corner.

Agent Fowler's jaw firmed, though he didn't contradict

his coworker. He pulled several pieces of paper from his portfolio. "We'll need a written statement regarding what happened from the time you found the thumb drive..." His eyes narrowed on Sunny. Agent Brown placed her hand on his arm again, and he continued, "From when you found the thumb drive until you knocked Larson cold."

Sunny accepted the papers and the pen the agent slid across the table to her, then flexed her hand, preparing to write quite a bit. "For the record, he knocked himself out. When I stepped aside, he tripped over my foot I left there on purpose."

"Cold, eh?" Cace smiled, pride practically radiating. "That's my girl."

CHAPTER 21

Sunny slipped the French wire through her earlobe and stepped back to survey herself in the hotel bathroom's wide mirror.

Nice. The pretty flowered dress clung to her curves, then flared out at her hips to swirl around her knees. The garment definitely didn't deserve to be on the clearance rack, but Sunny wouldn't question her luck. If Cace wanted to go to dinner at their favorite Italian restaurant tonight to celebrate their victory over the last couple of days, she would've worn a feed sack. She slid her feet into simple, strappy, sexy fuchsia sandals which highlighted some of the flowers in the dress. Also on clearance.

She hummed a happy little tune while she slicked gloss on her lips. One more glance.

No one would guess the day she'd had. Confronted Cary this morning. Wrote a never-ending statement for the VA agents. And finally, sat for an interview at Belton Police Department regarding Walter's stalking and attack. At least the pervert hadn't been able to retrieve the receiver, so he didn't see her and Cace make love or her naked at all. Too bad the same probably couldn't be said about the other victims on the thumb drive. Those poor women.

Anger started to leach in. Sunny pushed the emotion away. She and Cace were going to have a nice evening and forget about the last few days' chaos.

She stepped through the bedroom door and into the living area, where Cace straightened his tie.

Tie? And a blazer with his jeans and cowboy boots. A sexy combo with his still-damp, slicked-back hair. Her heart bumped, then began to beat a little faster at the sight. She blew a low whistle with a dramatic appraisal of his form. "Someone looks good tonight."

His lips quirked, and he took her in too. "Someone sure does. You ready?"

"Absolutely," she said. She reached for his proffered hand. He'd used the single word when Agent Fowler asked if he believed in her. No hesitation. No doubt in his tone. With that word, she couldn't have loved him more. The scene played over and over in her mind while they traveled to the restaurant. Hopefully, the wait wouldn't be too long to get a table since they didn't have a reservation—the place always booked up at least two weeks out, an oddity in Belton. Not surprising when the food would make an angel cry with happiness.

As soon as Cace gave his name, the maître d' gathered two menus and lead them to a spacious and very private u-shaped booth toward the back of the dining room. A lovely, low arrangement of flowers sat in the middle, unlike the simple buds on other tables. Had Cace arranged this? What was going on?

She slid into the banquette, scooting a bit until she turned the corner. Cace did the same. When they'd settled, a server brought a champagne bucket and, without comment, began to unwrap the bottle contained therein.

Sunny slid a side-eyed glance to Cace, who watched her, not the waitress filling the glasses.

"Take your time with the menu. I'll be back in a little while to take your order," the server said, then placed the heavy bottle back into the ice waiting in the bucket.

Cace handed Sunny one of the glasses.

"To what to I owe this luxury?" She canted her head a bit with the inquiry.

"You deserve this luxury each and every day."

She laughed and took a sip. Smooth and clean and bubbly. She'd never had champagne this good. "This doesn't taste like we can afford it every day."

"Then we'll save this for special occasions," he said with a casualness which was not at all casual.

Sunny's heart began to thump. "Special occasions?"

"Like today."

Oh. The bubbliness in her blood went flat. "Well, I guess you don't take down your stalker *and* catch a medical records thief every day."

The rare dimple, the one she so loved, popped into his cheek. "No, it's not. You constantly amaze me, Sunny. You intrigue me. You drive me crazy."

She fiddled with her glass's stem. "I know. And I'm sorry. I wish this silly Gift would leave me alone."

Cace shook his head. "Not that way. Crazy in love. With you."

Her heart skipped a beat, and she couldn't look away from the emotion shining in his eyes. "I love you too. More than you know."

"I hoped you did." He grasped her hand, and his thumb brushed back and forth over her knuckles. "I waited as long as I could. I know when I left you eight years ago, I was immature, and I broke your heart. We talked about taking our time to get to know each other again." His tone deepened. "I know you, Sunny, like my soul has always known yours and would find you in the world no matter the century. There's no other woman I would ever want to be with. I hope it's not too soon to ask."

He opened his other hand. In his palm lay a sparking ring, the central diamond encircled by small stones, which then swept down to encrust the setting and top half of the shank.

"Will you marry me?" The tiny bit of uncertainty peeking around his love almost undid her.

She swallowed, her eyes glued to the ring, the stones dazzling in the dim light. How could he doubt? "Of course I will marry you." Her words came out in a rush while her heart swelled with happiness. She hugged him hard, fitting her lips to his.

After a moment, he pulled back, a full-wattage grin on his face. "May I?" In his hand, he held up the ring.

She extended her fingers, not able to stop the fine trembling undoubtedly caused by the love and excitement of the moment. "Please."

The ring glided on—a perfect fit. She glanced down at the rainbow flashes. She wouldn't have cared if the ring had been made of fake gold, because she wouldn't have treasured it less. His love would be all she'd ever need.

He continued to hold her fingers gently, as if prized possessions he'd be afraid would break. "I am the luckiest man."

"To have a girlfriend with wacky powers who ends up in scrape after scrape and scares you half to death?"

"To have a woman with wacky powers who ends up in scrape after scrape and scares me half to death, yes. But one I know I must trust because she's smart and can take care of herself."

"I'm not that good yet," she said with a lopsided smile.

"I still might need a little saving." She paused. "From time to time."

"I hope we never have to do this again."

"I hope so too." She dropped her gaze to the ring as the stones flashed and winked, then back to the man she'd loved since the day in seventh grade when he told Brody Phillips to go sit on a cow's horn for calling her a 'Flannigan freak.' A smothered chime rang from her purse. In her bones she knew who sent her a text—her clairvoyant sister. Lacey's congratulations could wait.

Sunny had to clarify. "I can't promise the Gift won't put me in another scrape."

"I don't want any other promise except that you'll love me forever." No prevarication shaded the emotion shining in his eyes.

"That, Cace Navarro, I *can* promise." She wound her arms around his neck. "I will absolutely love you until the end of time."

Dear Reader,

Thank you so much for taking your time to read the Flannigan Sisters Psychic Mysteries series. Without readers, I wouldn't be able to do what I do, hopefully bring you fun, quick mystery reads with a touch of the paranormal.

Can I ask for a favor which takes you little time and no money? I would really appreciate a review of what you just read. A review not only helps other readers find books they'll love, but also helps the writer with visibility on book platforms and to get deals they can pass on to their fans.

Now for the good stuff! There are more Flannigan Sisters Psychic Mysteries novellas coming, so be sure to keep turning the page for an excerpt from *Gossip, Ghosts, and Grudges*, available Spring 2022!

Happy Reading,

Amanda Reid

Gossip, Ghosts, and Grudges
The *Flannigan Sisters Psychic Mysteries* Series
Book 8

A pie delivery to a B&B's grand opening party becomes a recipe for murder…

Haunted? Mina Flannigan laughs when one of her Dew Drop neighbors opens a small-town B&B and touts the house as spirit-occupied. How would Mina know things won't go bump in the night for guests? She can see ghosts, and them her.

Little does the B&B owner know that during an open house event, she'll get her opportunity for a real haunting when the town's most notorious gossip is found in the kitchen with a knife buried in her chest. With seemingly half of the town at the party and many of them with motive to kill the woman, the police's suspect list grows longer than the Rio Grande.

The very last thing Mina wants to do is help the annoying, gossipy ghost find the killer. But when the police add both an employee of Mina's diner and her best friend to the suspect list, she'll risk everything to ensure the two are cleared.

Mina best be discreet or risk running afoul of the real murderer…and joining the spirit world herself.

Get *Gossip, Ghosts, and Grudges* now, available exclusively through Kindle and Kindle Unlimited!

Want to know even more? Check out the first chapter by turning the page...

GOSSIP, GHOSTS, AND GRUDGES

CHAPTER ONE

Mina Flannigan Shaffer shut the back hatch of her SUV, biting her lip against an uncharacteristic swear word. Hefting two Sweetie's Tea Cup Cafe-branded pie coolers, one in each hand, she trekked from her house, across the street, then down three lots to Haunted Harlow House—correction—Dew Drop B&B.

While she crossed the short distance, she reminded herself to be thankful someone bought the Carpenter Gothic monstrosity. For eight years the home stood vacant, since Jolene Harlow died and left no descendants.

The once chipped and flaking paint on the elaborate trim had been remedied and missing bits restored so once again the steep, pitched gables and veranda roof appeared to drip with white lace. Gaps in the brick had been repaired, and shutters rehung.

Mina set one of the coolers on the concrete sidewalk and unlatched the gate to the white picket fence ringing the house. She carefully picked up the bag structured to carry three pies, and used her hip to shut the gate behind her. While the overgrown foundation plantings and trash trees had been cleared and replaced, they hadn't been able to save the walnut tree which had been planted when the house was built in 1870. The arborist had said, "Past its lifespan," when he and his crew removed the twisted, diseased carcass.

Once they'd removed walnut's giant, looming skeleton, the grim pall over the house lifted. Even before the trim's repainting, the town ceased using the title 'haunted'.

She set one of the coolers down and twisted the old-fashioned doorbell. The name change probably had the new owner worried. Anne Zaffuto marketed the house as a place to get your ghost on after gathering stories around the town. Many residents had sworn they saw faces in the windows or heard strange noises. Little did Anne or the rest of Dew Drop's population know, but there were no spirits in Harlow House.

Mina should know. She saw ghosts. And they her.

She repressed the urge to tap her booted toe with the delay. Finally, a shadow darkened the sheers-covered front door with its large inset beveled plate glass.

Anne swung the door open, dark brows gathered over the artsy purple frames of her glasses. "Mina. I thought you would've come to the rear."

The slight disapproving tone set her teeth on edge. Just because this town had a sleepy, lost-in-time atmosphere didn't mean Anne could treat people like the hired help. Somehow, Mina kept a snarky comeback behind her lips, opting for, "Your front door was closer and these are heavy."

She picked up the pie coolers and followed Anne down the central hallway to the back of the house. Mina set the coolers atop the soap-stone capped island. Once unzipped, she extracted the pies. "Here you are. Two Bacon Maple Butterscotch, two Blueberry Meyer Lemon chess and the Bourbon Chocolate Pecan."

Anne's eyes narrowed on the pies and she tucked a strand of her shoulder-length, salt-and pepper curls behind her ear. "Do you think I should've gotten more?"

Mina tamped down irritation at Anne's indecision. The woman initially groused at the cost of the specialty desserts and tried to wheedle a lower price by telling Mina featuring Sweetie's Tea Cup Cafe's pies at the opening reception for the B&B would be excellent advertising. Not likely. Mina could barely keep up after the Baking Channel's Southern Pie Master's debacle. Since Mina had helped to solve the mystery of who killed the channel's popular founder, the lines stretched out her restaurant's doors. More like Mina's pies would be the draw for Anne's reception.

Mina bit back the thought before the words tumbled out. It wouldn't hurt to be nice. "If you like, I can see where we are with pies today. I may be able to get you a couple more, I can't guarantee they'll be the same pies, though."

Anne tapped one of her index fingers tipped with a black nail against her fuchsia-tinted lips, probably calculating the cost-benefit. "Yes. Please. I have forty people invited. At eight slices a pie, even two more would make sure I don't run out."

"I'll check to see what we have." Doing the mental pie math of what she remembered being at the restaurant, she snagged her phone from the back pocket of her jeans. Anne better not ask for another discount. Luckily, three in the afternoon was a slow period and someone may be able to sneak away to deliver the pies.

Rageena Walton answered the phone at the Cup. With the extra business, Mina moved her reliable, turquoise eye-shadowed server to manager. "Looks like I could bring one of the pecan and one of the blueberry-lemon and we should have enough to get through the dinner service. I can be there in ten."

"Great—come to the back door, if you could." Though she hated make the request, no reason for Rageena to bear Anne's bad humor for not using the 'servant's entrance'.

Mina straightened her button-down, the one with the Cup's logo embroidered over her left breast, then moved around the three hired servers who'd arrived while she checked on pie availability. Via the wide hallway, she continued toward the front of the house, curious to inspect the rest of the house after its renovation. She could sneak in a couple of glimpses before Rageena arrived.

They'd really done an excellent job with the restoration, scraping away over one hundred years of dubious improvements to reveal the gem underneath. The staircase alone with its oak bannister would've taken months to redo, unless they'd sent the ornate wood away to be dipped to remove the paint. Mina stopped in the foyer to inspect the intricately molded newel post. Not a speck remained in the grooves and corners. Anne must've had the bannister professionally refinished.

"…don't care what you say," a voiced hissed. The words had floated in from over Mina's shoulder in the parlor. "You're a liar and I'm going to make sure you get what you deserve."

The sheer venom in the woman's voice shocked Mina, and she recoiled. Melissa Turner, aka Nosey. Mina would know the town's busybody anywhere. Ordinarily, she'd find the closest exit to avoid what with any other person would be a private moment, but listening to Nosey's divorce drama allowed for a little schadenfreude. Mina pushed aside any shame at her enjoyment. The woman had caused so much heartache for the people of Dew Drop.

"You're going to regret this," the distinctive rumble of

Jesse Turner's voice said, carrying an edge of fury. "I built the business from scratch, and you did nothing to support me. Except nag."

Nosey spit out a screech, then said, "I did no such thing. And if not for me, you wouldn't have a store. Maybe If you didn't carry on with every female employee, I might not be looking for half."

Half? Whoa. While not as successful as the more established Shaffer Hardware Mina's husband owned, Jesse had built Turner Hardware and Feed into a decent competitor. Suing for half in the divorce would be a blow. Poor guy, but then the two seemed to deserve each other.

Jesse swore, then heavy heels *thunked* on the floor.

Oh no. She couldn't be caught eavesdropping. Mina scanned for a place to hide, choosing to dart around the edge of the library's cased opening. The front door slammed and Mina let out a sigh of relief. She emerged back into the foyer at the same time as the other woman.

"Mina," Nosey exclaimed. One of her hands moved to cover where her light pink twinset met her throat, at the exact place where her grandmother's set of pearls lay. She wore the strand every day without fail. "I didn't know you'd be here for the reception."

A lie, though par for the course. Anne's invitation mentioned the event would be catered by XXBarbecueRestaurant with dessert by Sweetie's Tea Cup Cafe. Or maybe like Anne, she thought the 'help' too low to attend? Mina crossed her arms. "Good to see you too, Nosey."

Her cheeks reddened further, lips compressing to near non-existence. She'd always hated the nickname. And hated Mina, too. Nosey tossed her head as if to push her hair over her shoulder, except she wore it in a roll at the back of her head.

Though Mina had been trying to shed her mean-girl

tendencies, scoring a point with the woman caused a little surge of happiness, since Nosey never missed an opportunity for a gossipy or snide comment.

The front door opened, stalling Nosey's reply. Olivia Summers, Mina's best friend since first grade, entered the foyer. "Hi, Mina."

Goodness bless Olivia, she didn't even acknowledge Nosey, except for a scathing glare through narrowed eyes, before shifting her focus back to Mina. Olivia had to be one of the nicest people on Earth. That she'd stuck with Mina all these years should be enough proof for any jury. Bad enough Nosey had targeted Mina since she'd been in first grade and Nosey in sixth. Twenty-five years later, the annoying woman hadn't learned when to leave well enough alone. Even Olivia couldn't stand to be around her.

"Well hello there, Olivia." Nosey's head tipped back, assessing. "How's that son of yours doing? Repeating the third grade again, I hear."

Mina's sharply indrawn breath came out at the same time as her best friend's outraged hiss. Olivia stepped toward the awful woman and Mina grabbed her arm. Her friend shook off the restraint, and stayed put with lean forward. "One of these days, Melissa Turner, karma is going to give you your just desserts. And I hope I'm there to see it."

"Oh, you're going to see it," Mina said. Fury danced in her blood. Olivia's eight-year-old had a learning disability which had recently been diagnosed after years of struggle. Time to get ugly. "How about this?" She shifted to lean toward her friend, but maintained focus on the tall, waspish woman across from her. "Jesse has been sleeping with his female employees."

Nosey's hand flew to her pearls and her horrified

squeak echoed in the hall. She whipped her head in both directions probably to who might've overheard.

"I can't say I blame him," Olivia said, her tone tight and low. "As if anyone would find her attractive."

A muscle popped in Nosey's thin cheek and she jammed her fists on her gray, gaberdine pencil-skirt clad hips. "I'll have you know I receive plenty of male interest, thank you."

Doesn't even defend her husband. Figures.

"Stanley Jarvis doesn't count, since he'll sleep with anyone" Mina said, applying the smug satisfaction on thick. "You and he need to tone it down. You might as well have been carrying banners at the church anniversary party on Sunday."

Nosey froze, mouth half open, then snapped her jaw shut. "That's none of your business."

"Is the gander speaking?" Olivia asked, eyes wide with mock innocence. "I bet Gretchen Jarvis wouldn't be so excited to hear that little bit of gossip." She turned to Mina. "Though, I bet Jesse Turner might."

"Ooh," Nosey mumbled incoherently, cheeks bright crimson, then abruptly pivoted and stormed down the hallway toward the back of the house.

Though a vague worry of retaliation snaked through Mina, the gratification of a full-on victory wiped the feeling away. That woman deserved public humiliation and more.

"That's what I get for showing up on time," Olivia said, shaking her head. 'On-time' were words not generally associated with Olivia Summers and everyone in the town knew it.

Mina shot a cat-ate-the-whole-flock-of-canaries smile to her best friend. "But it was so satisfying to get to toss her life back at her. She's such a witch."

"I shouldn't let her get under my skin." Olivia smoothed down her western-styled blouse with a shaking hand.

Mina hated how the busybody had upset her friend. "Nosey could make the Pope cuss. You know that."

The front door opened and Mina moved to the side to get out of the way.

Speak of the horny devil. The City Manager, Stanley Jarvis, entered. He swept off his straw cowboy hat, revealing his deftly managed crop of thick, dark blond hair, a perfect complement to his blue eyes and wide, politician's smile. "Ladies," he said in passing. Anne emerged from the hall and swept him into the library.

Wouldn't Nosey's schnoz be out of joint if she saw the appraising way her lover's gaze swept over Anne's body. Mina snickered to herself, then sobered. Enough of letting the soon-to-be ex-Mrs. Turner get under her skin.

Mina stood by Olivia's side while in a matter of minutes, Anne had a full complement of Dew Drop's elected officials and business leaders, people probably more interested in what she'd done with Haunted Harlow House than anything else.

Stationed at the newel post, she and Olivia had a prime observation spot to survey the arrivals. At least until Olivia excused herself and wondered down the hallway in search of a bathroom. All attendees were known to Mina, and she became bored with her friend's departure. Her phone dinged and she checked the screen. Good. Rageena texted to say she'd delivered the pies and was headed back to the Cup.

Robert Ruiz strode through the door, bright gold shield on his belt next to the gun on his hip. A welcome sight. His arid sense of humor always delighted her.

She tucked her phone back into her jeans pocket. "Hey Chief. Didn't know you'd be here."

His mustache twitted with the lift of his lips. "Not going to miss an opportunity for a slice of your pie."

A laugh burst from her. "You had a slice of chocolate bourbon pecan with your chicken-fried steak at lunch."

He rubbed a hand over his stomach. "And I'm hoping you brought the butterscotch maple bacon."

"Anne asked for—"

An urgent, screeched "Oh my God," from down the hallway made Mina's head whip around. It had sounded like Rageena when she'd found a king snake in the cleaning closet. Not a sound of anger, one of pure terror.

Mina raced down the hallway toward the back of the house. Her boots skidded on the newly refinished oak floors and she grabbed the casing around the kitchen's door to stop from falling. Then her knees weakened, and her fingers dug in harder to keep upright and she stared at the figure on the floor, arms outstretched, mouth wide in a silent scream. The handle of a large knife protruded from the center of her chest. A surprisingly small crimson stain saturated the light pink twinset where the blade had been buried.

Mina's gaze shot to the only other person in the room. Rageena clutched the counter, eyes blown wide, mouth gasping for air.

Bodies crowded next to Mina, and Chief Ruiz's voice boomed over them. "Out of my way."

Mina's fingers clutched the molding, minuscule nails digging into the hard, ancient oak as if her only source of mooring. She tried to let go. Her hands seemed frozen and the lawman ended up shouldering his way around her.

"Oh my Goodness. Is that me?" Nosey's voice came from over Mina's shoulder.

She pivoted her gaze to over her shoulder. A black and white version of the woman on the floor stood behind Mina in the middle of the jostling on-lookers, one hand fingering the large pearl strand, lips pursed in the familiar judging, snooty expression.

Then the inappropriate thought zoomed through Mina's head—while Anne's house hadn't actually boasted a resident spirit in the past, the Haunted Harlow House now had its first ghost.

Get* Gossip, Ghosts, and Grudges, *the next fun adventure in the Flannigan Sisters Psychic Mysteries series, exclusively through Kindle and Kindle Unlimited!

ABOUT THE AUTHOR

Amanda Reid authors both the *Flannigan Sisters Psychic Mysteries* series and novellas in the *Enchanted Rock Immortals* paranormal romance series world. Since she was young, she's been a lover of mystery, sci-fi, romance, and paranormal books.

Beyond writing, Amanda was a career Army brat and lived in exotic locations like Tehran, Iran and DeRidder, Louisiana as a child. She obtained an International Politics degree and dreamed of a career in the State Department, but ended up as a federal agent. Amanda spent 24 years investigating murders, fraud, identity theft, drug dealers and many other crimes before retiring in mid-2019. As you can imagine, it's given her a wealth of inspiration for her mystery and urban fantasy stories.

She currently lives in Texas with her husband and two gonzo Australian Shepherds. Catch up with her on Instagram or Facebook. You can sign up for upcoming releases and promos at amandareidauthor.com.

Made in the USA
Columbia, SC
12 November 2024